W9-CMW-645

A SHERIFF FOR ALL
THE PEOPLE

A SHERIFF FOR ALL THE PEOPLE

JOHN REESE

DOUBLEDAY & COMPANY, INC.
GARDEN CITY, NEW YORK
1976

31993

All of the characters in this book are fictitious,
and any resemblance to actual persons, living or
dead, is purely coincidental.

Library of Congress Cataloging in Publication Data

Reese, John Henry.
A sheriff for all the people.

I. Title.
PZ3.R25673Shg   [PS3568.E43]   813'.5'4
ISBN 0-385-11011-1

Library of Congress Catalog Card Number 75-14839
Copyright © 1976 by John Reese
All Rights Reserved
Printed in the United States of America
First Edition

For Larry and Joyce Reese

A SHERIFF FOR ALL
THE PEOPLE

CHAPTER 1

Sheriff Rodgerson Downey, of Hillary County, Wyoming, slipped quietly out of bed that fall morning and went to the window that overlooked the front of his house. He had slept this night in the attic, as he usually did when he and his wife, Clytie, were on bad terms. His bare feet, flinching from the cold, unerringly found a squeakless route across the bare boards to the tiny front window.

There he squatted in his fleece-lined underwear, a burly man with a tangle of graying hair and a square, big-chinned face that needed shaving. He had always been a light sleeper, and he had awakened instantly upon the small squeal of the hinges on the door of the lean-to downstairs. The room adjoined the kitchen, and it was here that his boarder, Charley Noble, owner of the De Luxe Barber Shop, slept.

In a moment Downey saw the short, muscular figure of the barber walking sedately down the path with a bundle under his arm. Had Sheriff Downey not already known that this was Wednesday, he would have learned it now. Noble was not satisfied with a bath a week. No, he had built a bath house behind the De Luxe, where it was making him a small fortune, and he bathed on Wednesdays as well as Sundays.

Charley Noble carried his bundle of fresh clothing under his left arm. In his right, he carried the flat-topped, cavalry-style hat that he brushed so carefully each day. His chestnut hair was neatly combed in the middle. Even from behind, the points of his enormous, carrot-red longhorn mustache could be seen.

Charley walked like an old cowboy, in heeled boots into

which he had stuffed the pants that he would throw in the laundry after his bath. Although he was a businessman, a town man, he wore only cottons in his shop; wool caught too much hair. He could have been anywhere from twenty-five to forty. A man couldn't tell.

Sheriff Downey dressed hurriedly and went down the narrow stairs while pulling his suspenders over his shoulders. There was a chill here, too, but he did not take time to start a fire either in the kitchen range or in the stove in the living room. He slipped into his heavy saddle coat and clamped his hat down over his head.

"That you, Rodge?" came Clytie's sleepy voice.

"Who'd you think it was?" he replied.

"What are you doing up at this hour?"

"I got some letters to write for the early train. You'll have to milk the cow, and take the milk over to the Sontags."

"I usually do, don't I?"

"Well, so fur, it ain't hurt you none."

He closed the front door quietly and took his time on the path, not wanting to risk a meeting with his boarder if Charley had forgotten something and had to come back. The sheriff's little house was built on a hill that in the winter overlooked the town and in the summer was protected from the eternal wind by big, beautiful trees. He had three acres here. He kept a cow and five saddle horses. Clytie kept chickens and geese, and raised a big garden. He could smell the curl of smoke from the big smokehouse, where Clytie was curing six domestic geese, three wild ones, and nine ducks that Downey had shot, and a dozen big fish—trout and bass— that her Arapaho relatives had brought her in return for the gifts she was always giving them.

Clytie was supposed to be half Indian, although Downey was pretty sure in his own mind that her mother had been only half Indian herself. Clytie was hard-working, frugal, and a good housekeeper and cook. It had been a marriage of convenience for both of them, seven years ago, when Downey had been forty-eight and Clytie nineteen. Looking back, to Downey it seemed that the marriage had gone all to hell before it was two years old, when like a fool he had fallen in love with her.

He reached the street in time to see Charley Noble turn the corner. The sheriff turned a block earlier, to go through the back door of the courthouse, using his own key. He had one prisoner in his jail, a drifting cowboy by the name of Chet Wilson, doing thirty days for drunk and disturbing the peace. A nondescript, meek-looking man with a smart-aleck way of talking, Wilson was doing his time with a minimum of pain.

"Hidy, Sheriff. You must have a bad conscience," Wilson muttered from his blankets when Downey opened the door of his office. The cells—four of them—were behind the one big room where he had his desk.

"I might," Downey grunted, "and again, I might be just in a bad mood. So try your luck."

From the dark jail came a loud yawn. "When do we eat today, Mist' Sheriff?"

"You're going to eat at ten o'clock, as usual, and I'm going to eat when I get goddamn good and ready."

"Hope it's more of that good ol' cold oats with that good ol' skim milk."

The sheriff ignored that. He lighted a lamp that hung over his desk, unlocked the desk, and pulled out its bottom drawer. From the muss of papers there he pulled out a piece of paper. It was a "dodgeroo," sometimes known as a "wanted bulletin," and it had been out only a few months. It said, in big, black type:

TWO THOUSAND DOLLARS REWARD

will be paid by the Wyoming Bankers' Association, the Nebraska Bankers' Association, the Bankers' Protective

League of Colorado, and the Kansas Banking Institute, for the arrest and conviction, or for the delivery of the dead body, properly identified, of the notorious robber,

ROBERT EDWARD NYLANDER,

also known as "Chesty Bob," Bob Nelson, Bill Nelson, Jim Considine, etc. A master of disguise, this fugitive is also notoriously a quick-shot, cold-blooded KILLER! Description: 5 ft. 9 in., lithe build, eyes gray, green, or hazel, about 30 to 35 yrs. Has successfully posed as cattle broker, Army officer, book agent, mining engineer, and surveyor.

$2,000 reward—$2,000 reward—$2,000!

The sheriff's hand shook as he replaced the letter. "Chesty Bob" had stolen more than $165,000 from banks in four states in two years, working with never more than three confederates. He had killed two bank employees and one innocent bystander. It was also said that he had killed at least two, and probably three, of his own confederates, to beat them out of their shares.

A master of disguise, was he? What better disguise was there than the barber's trade, a red steerhorn mustache, and an air of fawning stupidity? Who knew where Charley Noble, master barber, came from? Where had the cash come from to buy the rundown De Luxe last fall, repaint it, and install the boiler and bath house in the room behind? And where better to get the information a bank robber would need than from the sheriff's wife?

If the son of a bitch has seduced Clytie, Downey thought, I ain't going to arrest him. I'll kill him and sell his body for the reward. . . . Suddenly the sheriff lost all heart, all enjoyment of life. He dropped his head and buried his face in his arms on the desk, and something inside him where his heart belonged cried, *Why, Clytie, why? It was so good at first—what happened?*

● ● ●

The political bug had bitten Rodgerson E. Downey late in life. All his life he had been one of the humble ones, thinking himself lucky indeed to have a steady job as foreman on a fine place like Hugh Dean's HD ranch. Rodge (to his friends, who had never been numerous) had given way to ambition strictly by accident, when a cousin of Hugh's came out from Ohio eight years ago to spend the summer on a real cow-outfit.

"Downey, is it?" said the cousin when he was introduced to the foreman. "That's a good name, you know."

"Good for what?" its owner replied.

"I think in political terms, you know, that being my lifetime career. There are some names that win elections, you know, because they seem to charm and comfort the voter."

"Is that right!"

"Yes, and Downey is high on the list. Other good political names are Walker, Graves, Howard, Ballew, Bradley, and Carpenter. On the other hand, men named Anderson, Perkins, Peebles, Ludlow, Reese, or Beasely are very, very difficult to elect."

The foreman had narrowed his eyes suspiciously. "Aw, you're making fun of me!"

"Oh no! I assure you, there are good political names and bad ones, and Downey is one of the best. What's your first name?"

"Rodgerson, with a *d*."

"You really must consider running for office! I have never heard a better political name than Rodgerson Downey. You would have to get married, of course. If you were a young man you could get by without that. People would assume that you would get married sometime. But a man of your mature years who is still a bachelor is a bad example. The men envy him and their wives distrust him. You may take my word for it that you make a good appearance—solid, strong, with a good, straight gaze and a resonant voice. People would trust you, but you have to ask them, you know. You have to make the race yourself."

Only a casual conversation, yet it stirred something in Rodge Downey that he had never dared to feel before. But how did a man start a political career?

Downey's chance came less than a week later, when Hugh Dean was grumbling about something the veteran sheriff of Hillary County had done. "Damned old fool, he should've been put out to pasture years ago, but he's been in there so long, nobody dares to run against him," Hugh said.

"Maybe," Downey gulped, "I will."

"You sure don't figger to do no worse than him."

"Listen, Hugh—"

The cattleman had other things on his mind, but Downey made him listen to what his own cousin had said. Downey could see Hugh's face get crafty. He began to nod and scowl and bite his lip.

"What bothers me," Downey said, "is who I'd marry. I'd be willing, if I could find somebody. Hugh, I know just about everybody in the county. I never been in trouble here. All my life I been a nobody. This is the best job I ever had, but—"

Hugh interrupted, in that overbearing way of his, to say, "How about that Tate girl?"

"What Tate girl?"

"You never seen Clytie Tate? She must be eighteen or twenty by now."

"That's too young for me."

"It ain't never too young if the girl betters herself. Let's think this over, Rodge. If you decide it's the thing to do, I'll talk to old Tate. Then some night you shave up and put on some clean pants and shirt and socks, and you ride over and take that girl some kind of a present. Buy her a lace handkerchief or something. The more I think of this, Rodge, the better I like it!"

And so he had married Clytie Tate. No one had bothered to tell him that she had Arapaho blood in her and could be as proud and mean as a chief. Nobody had warned him that a quiet, pretty girl with downcast eyes could turn into a she-wolf who would just as soon hit you over the head with a skillet as not. Above all, no one had prepared him for the battle of silence, which a woman always won.

The lieutenant governor was not going to run again next election. He was taking a job as a United States judge, leaving a vacancy not everyone knew about. Those who did took it for granted that the job would go to a Cheyenne lawyer—a good lawyer, a man well known throughout Wyoming, and a peerless orator.

But—and Rodge Downey knew this, whether anyone else did or not—Sam Drake, the peerless candidate, *could be beaten!* Drake was having wife problems. Downey did not know exactly what kind they were, but his information was that the marriage was on the rocks. A man who had already won three county elections, say, a mature old-timer who captured the most notorious bank robber since Jesse James, could whip Sam Drake easily and soundly.

But not, of course, if he was having wife problems of his own.

Downey slipped the dodgeroo back into his desk, locked the desk, and went outside, locking the courthouse behind him. He crossed an empty street, impervious to the beauty of the town in the predawn light. He walked swiftly down the six-foot space between the Hillary National Bank and the Sontag Mercantile Company. Behind the two buildings was an eight-foot plank fence, with a plank gate held by a chain and padlock.

The sheriff took out several keys. He had borrowed them

from Erik Sontag only last evening. "A Gleason and Fitch brand padlock, about yea big," he said, measuring it with his hands.

"That's a number fourteen. They make about a dozen key fittings. I can let you use what I've got in stock, Rodge," said Erik. He did not ask the sheriff why he needed a key. He was a law-abiding man, glad to assist.

The first key fit. Downey quietly removed the chain, slipped through, and put the chain and padlock on the ground. He was in a small back yard, much of which was taken up by the woodshed that now housed the boiler and bath. The shed had no lock.

Downey slipped into it and closed the door behind him. He was in the boiler room. There was a new partition between it and the new bath. He groped his way stealthily to the partition. Just as he knelt down at the knothole, it glowed yellow as Charley Noble lighted a big lamp, and then another, in the bath room.

Downey applied his eye to the knothole and saw his boarder leaning over to start the water gurgling into the big galvanized tub. Outside, a windmill creaked as the automatic trip in the tank on the roof let it turn into the wind. The pump began pulsing. With two sets of pipes carrying moving water, Downey could forget noise.

Noble spread his clean clothing out on a bench and began to undress. His upper body was not heavy, but it was muscular. Charley had no hint of a belly. And as Charley stepped out of his underwear, Downey suddenly remembered the old story about the bank-walker who ran off with the fellow's wife.

"I don't believe I know any such person," said a friend. "In fact, I don't even know what a bank-walker is."

"You don't?" said the betrayed husband. "Didn't you ever go swimming in the crick? There's always some that shuck off their clothes fast, and then holler, 'Last one in is a piece of cheese!' But there's always somebody that takes his time, and then walks up and down the bank a long time after he's undressed, before he goes into the water. Well, my wife ran off with a goddamn bank-walker!"

Charley Noble could qualify. This was not what the sheriff had been trying to determine, but maybe it was important. Charley shut off the water and turned his back to inspect his big, handsome mustache in a mirror. Downey felt another tug of excitement. Was it a false one, part of one of Chesty Bob's famous disguises?

No, the way he tugged and tweaked and twisted it, that was real enough. But then the sheriff's heart gave a choking leap as he saw Charley lift his entire scalp from his head and lay it carefully aside. Under it, he was as bald as a baby's butt, except for a fringe around the sides and a screen down the back of his neck.

A wig, a toupee! And an expensive one that had cost twelve or fifteen dollars! Real human hair, the right shade to go with his mustache, and what a different man he was without it!

Charley eased himself into the hot tub. "Ahhh," he sighed. Downey stood up, felt his way out of the shed, and closed the door behind him. He locked the gate after he had passed through, thinking, I've got him! Got the worst bastardly bank robber since Jesse James! All I have to do is squeeze down at the right moment, and smash him like a bedbug. And then let's see what Clytie says. . . .

CHAPTER 2

Clytie was milking the cow when Downey got back to the house. Coffee was ready, but not breakfast. He drank a cup of scalding coffee, standing in the kitchen, and then got out his things to shave. He was shaving when his wife came in with the milk.

"Why ain't breakfast ready?" he asked her.

"I ain't running a restaurant. You usually don't eat here," she replied.

"The reason why, I always have to wait on it."

"You could fix it yourself."

Clytie easily swung the heavy milk pail to the table, got out her clean crocks, and carefully strained the milk into them. The cow had come fresh in September and was giving them better than two gallons to the milking.

"Don't you take the Sontags their milk before you set it out for the cream to raise?" Downey asked.

"I ain't waiting on the Sontags. They send one of their kids up when they want milk."

Count on her to say exactly the wrong thing at the wrong time. Just when a man was at the most important crisis of his career, she had to get one of her Indian grudges against a man who could be important. The sheriff's habitually careful grip on his temper loosed suddenly. He whirled on her with the razor in his hand.

"Damnit, I made a deal with them to deliver half a gallon of milk every day before breakfast!"

"And I made one for them to send a kid up here. If you want it delivered, you deliver it."

He had to make a powerful effort to keep from striking at her with the razor in his hand. Not that he could have hurt her. Clytie was quick as a mink, and lately about as wild and mean. She baited him into hitting her, and then threatened to kill him if he did. So far, he had not laid hands on her.

Clytie took after both ancestral strains in a curious way, as did all the Tate kids. Her hair was almost fair. Her face, with the summer's tan on it, was golden or tawny. Her eyes were huge and dark under dark, heavy eyebrows. Her figure was slim and straight-backed. Her bare feet, under the hem of her old gray dress, were small, high of arch, and somehow touchingly pretty.

He ached for her love, her friendship, even her toleration. But then he remembered that stud of a barber, and wanted to cry. He pointed to her feet.

"Where are your shoes, woman? What have I told you about running around barefoot?"

"Look at my shoes, why don't you?"

"What about your shoes?"

"Ha! A pair of dancing shoes too small for me, that you bought because they was cheap. A pair of boy's shoes to garden and milk in! Listen, Rodge, I don't put on shoes again until I pick them out myself. I ain't going to wear anything— not *anything*—without I pick it out myself."

He never had been able to get her to buy things for herself. She was shy about going into stores and being waited on by men; and as for spending money, oh lord, there wasn't anybody in the world as tight as Clytie! How could she blame him for not having shoes?

Well, now he knew. That goddamn bank-robbing barber was why. "Then," he said thickly, "you can damn well go naked."

"I won't mind, if you don't. I don't care who looks at my nakedness."

He dropped his razor on the table and lunged at her blindly. She seemed to glide just out of his reach. He started after her. Clytie picked up a folded dish towel to use as a pad, and laid hold of the handle of the coffeepot. She was always threatening to scald him, and she'd do it, too.

He stopped, defeated. "Clytie, for Christ's sake, why do you have to devil me so early in the morning? I've got worries you don't even know about. Why can't you help a man, instead of always being against me?"

"Here come the Sontag girls for their milk."

It was creepy, how she could hear two barefoot girls so far away. Sometimes he swore she could hear a butterfly trying its muscles from a mile away. He picked up his razor and went on shaving. Clytie filled the syrup pail with milk for the two little tow-haired girls, and sent them on their way cheerfully.

"Don't you trip and spill it, now, or you kids won't get any breakfast, you hear?"

The girls went out. Downey could hear the calf bawling in its pen, and any sound drove him crazy this morning. "You mean to starve that calf to death, or what?" he demanded, wiping off the last of the lather.

"Who you want fed first, you or the calf?"

"Skim the milk. I'll feed it."

When he turned, she was already skimming last night's milk. "I'll feed it. Do you want breakfast now, or don't you?"

"For God's sake, I'll eat at Tong Ti's!"

"Well, change your shirt. You look like a pig."

"Oh lordie, lordie," he moaned softly.

He changed his shirt and went back down the hill to the courthouse. His kid deputy, Monte Barrett, had fed his own horse and the one Downey kept in the stable behind the courthouse, and was sweeping out the office. Monte was twenty-three or -four, and the father of a year-old girl, but he looked like a weedy schoolboy. Tangled red hair, big nose, watery blue eyes, dressed always in shabby, patched clothing, he lived in terror of losing his job. His wife had to work as a waitress in Tong Ti's, leaving the baby with her mother. What they did with their money, Downey could not imagine.

Clytie would have saved half of what the two of them earned.

Monte blinked at Downey helplessly. "Prisoner is hollering for his grub, Sheriff."

Downey unlocked his desk and took out a Colt .45 in a holster. "I'll bring him something from the Chinyman's. You clean this gun up good, and oil the belt."

"You bet!"

"Fill every loop in that belt with a cartridge, and six in the gun. You can handle a shotgun, can't you?"

"Sure. I ain't much of a wing shot, but—"

"I want you to take the twelve-gauge out, and a box of shells, and shoot up the whole box until you can hit what you aim at. You've got a forty-five, ain't you?"

"Yes, only I can't afford—"

"You wear it in the future. I'll buy your shells. From now on, it's a rule around here that both of us go armed except when we're in our own houses. A peace officer is on duty twenty-four hours a day, and don't you forget it."

In the jail behind the office, the prisoner began playing his harmonica, searching for a tune—and how he could play it! In the old days Downey had been pretty good with a mouth organ, but not this good, nor had he ever had so fine an instrument. He listened for a moment, grinning at Monte.

"Hey, that's a nice tune, boy," he called when it ended. "What's the name of it? How does it go?"

The disturber of the peace sang raucously:

"Old man Dan, he ran and ran
So he'd be there when the fight began.
Now old man Dan and the other man,
They both gotta do three months in the can.
For he was too durned fast, just too durned fast. . . ."

"I never heard that one before," Downey said.

"How about this one?" The prisoner did not bother to seek out the tune on his harmonica before singing:

"Oh, I pray I'll see you, Mother,
In the sweet bye-and-bye.
And it won't be very long, Mother,
For I'm so hungry I could die."

Downey laughed, his good humor restored. "All right, cowboy, let's see what the Chinyman can do with a mess of pancakes and eggs. How does that sound?"

"Yay, that sounds great. Geewillickers, I'll hate to leave here, you keep this up, Sheriff."

Downey could handle humble people, and he knew it. He took no nonsense from prisoners or deputies, but neither did he make them feel more humble still. He had also developed confidence in himself with other county officials, and when the county treasurer stopped him in the hall, the sheriff handled him, too. All he had to do was get out his little pocket notebook.

"There's a voucher for sixty-four dollars and seventy cents somewhere, Ted. Here's the number—two, three, two, zero, six, Series B three. Zack Snively's taxes. I had to let him have fifteen of my own money to make it, poor old bastard, so I ain't going to be mistaken about this one. You just didn't get this one posted, but you bet your bottom dollar I've got your receipt for it."

"I won't argue with you on that," the treasurer said, making a memorandum of the voucher number. "You're good with figures and you're good with people, Rodge."

"I just do my job."

"Thing I like about you, Rodge, you ain't just a weapon-heavy brawler. You treat rich and poor alike. You're a sheriff for all the people."

For some incomprehensible reason, a gush of some kind of excitement came up in Downey's throat, choking him. He wished that Clytie could have heard Ted Snively say that. He did not try to speak over the lump in his throat. He merely thumped Ted's arm and grinned and went on.

Sheriff for all the people. It was a new idea. If Ted was going around saying that behind his back, it would make people appreciate him. Everybody but my wife, Downey thought bleakly. Everybody but Clytie . . .

Tong Ti's place was full. A couple of cattlemen had brought their big families in, to catch the morning train to Cheyenne, and all the tables were full. The only seat at the counter was next to Downey's boarder, Charley Noble, now secretly known to Downey as Chesty Bob Nylander. Downey would rather have sat down beside a rattlesnake, but he hung his hat on a peg and took the creaking stool.

"How come you didn't eat at the house, Charley?" he said. "You paid for room and board, didn't you?"

"Oh, hidy, Mr. Downey," Charley said. "I just didn't want to make no extra trouble for Clytie, with her milking and chickens and everything. Anyway, I wasn't on time. This is bath day for me, you know."

"Well, if you want to throw your money away, I can't stop you."

Monte Barrett's wife, Lena, stopped in front of Downey. She was a chubby girl, pale of hair, and so fair-skinned that her body would surely be as white as milk. Yet there was a smoky look behind her eyes that made Downey sure there was fire in her somewhere. She could make a seductive exercise out of pouring a cup of coffee.

"More coffee, Mr. Noble?" she said in that soft voice of hers. "What'll you eat, Sheriff Downey?"

"Oh, I reckon bacon and eggs."

"Eggs soft, with fried potatoes."

"You know by now, don't you?"

"I ort to." Her eyes kept straying back to Charley. "Everything all right with your breakfast, Charley?"

"Real fine, ma'am."

She reached behind her for a cup and saucer and filled the cup for Downey. She swayed on down the counter, her full hips writhing under her faded dress. Downey had never given her a thought before, but her attentiveness to Charley Noble called her to his attention. This damned bank robber with his wig had every woman in town eating out of his hand, looked like.

"A nice young lady," Charley sighed.

"Yes, and her husband is my deputy and he goes armed," Downey said.

"I know. They make a nice little family, them two and their little girl. I never had no truck with kids, to speak of, but they got a real cute young'n."

"Yes, she's cute."

"You ever have any kids, Mr. Downey?"

"Now, that's a funny thing for you to say, Charley. You live right in the house with me."

"Well, I thought maybe you'd been married before, or something."

"You mean I look that goddamn aged to you?"

"Why should I think something like that?" Charley exclaimed in a shocked voice.

Downey did not answer, but pitched into the plate of breakfast that Lena brought him. What, he worried, had made Charley ask something like that? He remembered that there was no such person as "Charley Noble," that he was sitting beside Chesty Bob Nylander, the worst bastardly bank robber since the James Boys. A planner, everybody said. A crafty, cold-blooded thinker who went into a robbery with a cat at every rat-hole.

Downey was glad when someone put a hand on his shoulder and said, "Howdy, Sheriff. Me and the family is going to Cheyenne for a few days. Don't you let nobody rob us blind while we're gone."

It was one of the cattlemen. Downey reached up and patted the hand on his shoulder. "You be damn sure of that," he said.

"Last thing we worry about, with you on the job."

The cattleman gathered up his family and left the cafe, and the sheriff for all the people pulled himself together. Lena Barrett stopped before him.

"Your breakfast to your liking, Sheriff?"

"Well, the eggs didn't seem too fresh, Lena."

"Sheriff, them eggs is so fresh that the hens are still receiving congratulations."

It took him a moment to get it. He rewarded her with a deep, spontaneous chuckle. "Lena, I'm going to have to tell Monte that there's too many fresh traveling men here. You're getting too fast for our company."

"Ain't nobody gets ahead of you, though, I reckon," she drawled. She refilled his coffee cup and departed, a blinding vision of hips that would be oh, so white and firm and—

"Back to work. Another day, another dollar," Charley Noble was saying. "A million days, a million dollars."

Charley stood up. Downey pushed back his plate, his mind made up. It was time to snuggle up to this fellow a little. Be friendly, learn what he could, let the bank-robbing bastard think he was fooling everybody.

"You know what I think, Charley? I think it's time I had my hair cut."

"You come in when you're ready and I'll make sure everybody knows you're next up."

"Appreciate that."

Charley walked, Downey noticed, on the balls of his feet, light on the heels, ready to jump like a cat. He sort of slithered, boots and all. Good man with his fists, Downey was sure. Oh, the sly son of a bitch!

Tong Ti came to the door to pay his respects when Downey left, a moment or two later. Downey knew better than to embarrass them both by trying to pay. All you did was call attention to things, with a two-bit bluff like that. Tong was not just a businessman who protected his own interests. He was a friend, too.

"You put up a real good meal here, Tong," Downey said.

"We always do our best for our sheriff." Unlike many of his race, Tong had no difficulty sounding an *l*.

"We all do our best here, Tong. That's why it's a good town to live in."

"You never said truer words. In the Book of Isaiah it is written, 'I have raised him up in righteousness, and I will direct all his ways, he shall build my city and he shall let go my captives, not for price or reward, saith the Lord of hosts.'"

"Do tell!"

It was a day for learning things—first, that his boarder was a bank robber, and now that Tong Ti was an educated Bible-reader. The sheriff felt ignorant and uncouth. Next, he'd be feeling beaten down and worthless again. Time to pull himself together.

There were two ways he could handle this business, he thought moodily, walking slowly back to the courthouse. One way, he could bide his time, catch Charley as he made his jump, and harvest all the credit for it. With just one good deputy to help him, that would be the thing to do.

But the county was too tight to pay for a good man. Monte Barrett got twenty-five dollars a month, plus free use of a shacky little old house that the county had taken over for nonpayment of taxes. What you got for that kind of pay was . . . Monte Barrett.

The other way was to go to the president of the Wyoming Bankers' Association and make him a proposition. The very thought sent chills through Downey. The head of the WBA was Mr. Jerome Follansbee, president of the Merchants and Drovers Bank of Curtin, Wyoming. Downey had met him a couple of times. Follansbee was so old that he creaked when he walked. He knew everybody. He knew everything there was to know about anything.

Follansbee had even been to England twice, free. His bank was trustee for some kind of a big English lord who had a cattle ranch that sprawled clear up into the mountains. He was not likely to pay much attention to a minor sheriff.

Downey forgot all about bringing breakfast to his prisoner. He went straight to the barber shop, which was not yet open. He hammered on the door, and Charley Noble skipped nimbly to open it. He uncovered the chair with a flourish, spread the apron between his hands like a bullfighter with his cape, and let Downey sit down.

"How do you want it cut, Mr. Downey?"

"You're the barber. Just whack away until you're sure it ain't an old bull buffalo in your chair."

Downey watched a new man emerge in the mirror. He had never minded his gray hairs, but neither had he realized how a mass of them could age him. It was a younger, more forceful man the sheriff beheld. Meanwhile, Charley Noble prattled away.

"I never went to no barber school, you know. I was working on a spread in Idaho, and I sprained a knee. Couldn't work, and I had plenty of time to think how I was wasting my life. Teamster, tunnel-mucker in a mine, and plenty of pick-and-shovel jobs. You know how it goes."

I sure do, the sheriff thought, but I doubt if you do. . . .

"So I took what I had saved up, and I paid this barber fifty dollars to learn me the trade, and then I worked for him a year or two. So that's how I got to be a barber, and a pretty good one, if it is me that says it."

"How'd you happen to light here, and where did you get the money to buy the De Luxe and put in that bath house and boiler?"

"Why, I had about eight hundred saved up, and then an old aunt back in Missouri, she died and left me about fifteen hundred. Then I had some guns I didn't need—I's always a fool for guns—and I sold them and a couple of horses I had. Now just let me slosh on some of this lilac tonic, and you're a new man, Mr. Downey."

And not a bad-looking one, either. He was glad that Clytie had made him change his shirt. Squaring his shoulders in the mirror, fitting his hat down over the handsomely combed and parted hair, the prospect of facing down Jerome Follansbee in his office seemed somehow less remote. The problem was to get there. The county would not pay his fare without a better reason than he could supply, and Clytie would just raise hell.

CHAPTER 3

"You said you's going to bring me some pancakes," Chet Wilson wailed.

"I plumb forgot," the sheriff confessed.

"Sure, what is it to you whether I starve to death or not? And look at this leg, Mist' Downey. It's festering up on me under that scab."

Downey went to the bars to look. He took off his gunbelt and keys and handed them to Monte Barrett. "Lock me in and wait here."

He went into the cell. Wilson pulled up the leg of his Levi's. He howled when Downey prodded the inflamed area with his finger.

"Kee-rist, I told you it's festering. That hurts!"

"I can well believe it does," Downey said, "but you got that resisting arrest, and look here—if you's working in somebody's roundup camp, you wouldn't miss a day in the saddle, would you?"

The woebegone cowboy pulled down his pants leg and grinned sheepishly. "All right, turn me loose and I'll go get a job."

"You rattle-headed riders is all alike. You try to wreck somebody's saloon and whip the sheriff, and then you want somebody to feel sorry for you because you got a little scratch doing it. Break that scab and wash it out with yellow soap. That's all a doctor can do."

Wilson lay back and covered his eyes with his arm. "Mist' Sheriff, I don't want to lose that leg, and if that greens up with blood poison, that's what's going to happen to it. I'll be a one-legged man."

Poor devil, Downey thought, I used to be just as meek and humble, and no more sense. And by God, if I'm a sheriff for all the people, I'm the sheriff of these poor ignorant cowboys, too. . . .

"Can you walk, Wilson?"

"Sure. You going to send me to the doctor?"

"I reckon."

Wilson sat up eagerly. "I had a dollar or two on me when you locked me in. How about a shave and a haircut, too? With some of that stinkwater you got on. I smell like a damn billy-goat."

"That's from not taking a bath." Downey thought it over. "Tell you what I'm going to do. I'll have Mr. Barrett handcuff your right wrist to his left one. He'll take you to breakfast at Tong Ti's, and then to the doctor, then to the barber shop. Mr. Barrett won't have no gun on, so don't get no ambitious idees. If you so much as look crosswise, I'm going to pound you flat."

"My stars, only nineteen days to go, and you think I'd try to break jail?"

"No, or you sure as hell wouldn't go." Downey made a sign to Monte, who unlocked the cell door. "Monte, there's three dollars and thirty cents in the cash box. Take vouchers along for Doc Lavoey to sign. I'll stand treat for his breakfast—yours too, if you're hungry."

"I could eat." Monte gulped. "But I don't know as I want to be chained to him while he's getting a shave and haircut. You remember Mamie Boyle."

Mamie Boyle, the cook in the Hillary Hotel, had been attacked by a rapist a few months back. She had managed to get to her scissors before it was too late. She had quite efficiently driven one point of them into the attacker's throat, making it unnecessary for the sheriff to kill him.

"He won't need no scissors, Mist' Downey," the prisoner

said piteously. "Just shear me off like a sheep. Could I have a bath, too?"

"You really want room service, don't you? Snub up short here while I go see if the doctor wants you this morning."

Dr. James Lavoey's office was less than a block away. He suggested that the prisoner be bathed before coming in for treatment. Charley Noble agreed to take Wilson at any time. "I won't bill you for the bath, Mr. Downey. The water's already hot, and I wouldn't impose on the taxpayers like that."

No, all you'd do is rob the bank or anything else you could get your hands on. . . . Downey returned to the courthouse and dispatched a grateful prisoner and an apprehensive deputy, securely chained together, on their errand of mercy and hygiene. Monte had brought the morning mail, which was on his desk. He ran through it without much interest.

Horse thief wanted. Wife-murderer wanted in Oklahoma. California man wanted for murdering a mail rider. Another horse thief. Post office robber. Downey studied each conscientiously, but they were all cheap outlaws compared with Chesty Bob Nylander.

There was one letter for Clytie, from her relatives in Omaha. He opened it and skimmed through it. Her paternal grandmother was expected to die, and wanted to see Clytie before she went. He tossed it aside angrily, thinking what a hell of a nerve they had, to expect him to pay her fare back for that.

Then he snatched up the letter again and read it more carefully. If he went too, and paid their own way, it was an excuse to take an eastbound train! He could find some way to get off at Curtin, and either come home again after seeing Jerome Follansbee or catch the next train to Omaha.

Rodgerson Downey had always been frugal because he had never had the money to be anything else. Clytie had taught him how to accumulate money, how to acquire things without spending. He had an account in the bank that was earning a steady eight per cent. His house and lot were paid for.

He owned five horses, a cow, and a collection of pistols, rifles, and shotguns. If he died tomorrow, Clytie would be fixed for life.

To take more than a month's pay out of the bank was not a step to be taken lightly. Neither could he let this chance slip away. First, he had to find out just how much it would cost on the train for Clytie and himself.

People spoke to him, and some even touched their hats, as he hurried down to the Union Pacific depot. He seemed to meet more people on the street than he usually did—or perhaps he was merely more aware of them, since lifting his eyes to the illuminated elevation of the lieutenant governor's office. He had always known that he had friends here, despite being a standoffish man. But he had never realized just how many, until now.

Even the Indians who always collected around the depot grinned and nodded to him, and not just because he had married a woman with Indian blood, either. He could cross the tracks to where a dozen or so women made a precarious living at the oldest of trades and find friends there, too. He kept them off the streets except on Monday afternoons, at the hours decent women were home fixing supper for their loved ones, and yet they liked him.

And why not? He was their sheriff, too, wasn't he?

He had stopped the thieving of cattle, the fighting in town by cowboys, and their vulgar street talk that, in the past, had offended the decent women. He checked the brand of every strange horse that came to town, and had caught three horse thieves that way. There hadn't been a burglary or even a clothesline robbery for years.

He had never realized it until this morning, but law enforcement was a trade, and he always had gone about it with a queasy inner determination to do the best he could. No one, he saw now, had ever suspected how unsure of himself he had been. He had asked questions of other sheriffs, of federal marshals. His one hope had been that people might *respect* him, if they never feared or liked him.

If only Clytie didn't make life so miserable! A sullen, glowering, pouting, bad-tempered, barefoot squaw as the wife of the lieutenant governor? Oh, lordie . . .

Someone was in the office with the station agent and Downey had to rap on the wooden ledge at the ticket window to get his attention.

"Dogged if I wasn't just talking about you, Sheriff Downey," the agent said. He leaped up to unlock and open the door. "Here's a man wants to see you. It's my pleasure to introduce you to Louis Varden, chief of protection for the Union Pacific. Mr. Varden, this is our sheriff, Rodge Downey."

Downey shook hands with a well-dressed, limber-looking man of about forty-five. Hazel eyes with the glint of a trapped bobcat's. Long jaw, down-turned mouth, a couple of gold teeth, and a scar across one temple that had almost cost him an ear.

Railroad dicks were rarely liked by anyone, especially local peace officers. They thought themselves too smart, and their railroads too powerful. What they asked for, they expected to get. This Louie Varden was probably the best-known man in his dubious trade; and to Downey he looked like a man easy to dislike. Easy to fear, too, if you happened to be his adversary.

"I came here especially to talk to you. Wonder where we could chat in absolute privacy?" Varden said in a wonderfully low and mysterious voice.

"How about my office?"

"A sheriff's office is usually pretty busy."

"Mine ain't, not today. Come along."

This Varden actually took hold of Downey's elbow, like a long-lost relative. Outside, on the cinder platform, a big, slab-sided cowboy whose name Downey could never remember had cornered a couple of Indian boys against a box car. He was almost middle-aged, and the Indian kids were sixteen, seventeen, something like that. The cowboy wore a .45 in a holster buckled up high on his hip, on the side. The Indians were unarmed—except, of course, for the inevitable barlow folding knives that all boys carried.

"I can't imagine a belly without a bellybutton," the cowboy was saying. "Pull out your shirt and show me what an Indian's belly looks like without one."

"You let me alone," one of the boys said.

The cowboy made a grab at his shirt. The boy slid aside with the lightning grace that, in Clytie, both baffled Downey and stirred a mystical excitement and admiration in him. The cowboy turned, caught the other, smaller boy by the arm, and with his other hand pulled at his shirt.

"Just show me," he said.

"Excuse me, Mr. Varden," said Downey.

Four long, fast, running steps took him to the side of the cowboy. An elbow in the stomach doubled the cowboy up, and when he reached for his gun Downey hit him in the back of the neck with a hard, clubbed fist. Down went the cowboy, the Indians on top of him, blubbering in their throats with rage.

Downey caught them by the hair, one boy in each hand, and yanked them back. They tried to ignore him and go for the cowboy again. He slammed them together, hard, and then slammed them back against the box car.

"You hold everything, now! I won't have no fights, you understand that?"

"Mr. Rodge, you know what he said to us?" one of the boys said seethingly.

"I know. You go on about your business, now, and let me take care of him."

"No! He ain't going to pick on me no more."

"No, he ain't, but I'm going to paddle your asses good if

you don't get the hell out of here. What are you loafing around the depot for, anyway? If all you can do is get into fights, stay out of town!"

The other Indians were watching, grinning under the hats that hid their dark faces. He shoved the boys hard, to give them a running start, and turned his back on them. The cowboy was perfectly conscious, but his eyes still had a little blur in them. Downey hauled him to his feet by his shirt front, with both hands, and stood him against the box car.

"What's your name, ranny?"

"Joe Ogren. You know me, Sheriff. I—"

"Your damn right I do. You working now?"

"No, I's laid off last week, six of us. We—"

"Then get the hell out of the town of Hillary."

"Listen, you can't run me out of town like a vagabond. I got over eighty dollars in my pocket."

Ogren stood four inches higher than the sheriff, outweighed him by thirty pounds, and had twenty years' advantage in age. Downey slapped him so hard that the thud of his head against the box car echoed through the whole car. Ogren's eyes went blank again and his knees buckled. Downey held him on his feet and against the box car with his left hand, keeping his right fist cocked.

"What the hell is this? Are you arresting me?" the cowboy said, when he had his wits back and could say anything.

"The likes of you? I told you to get out of town, didn't I? Does that sound like arresting you? Listen, you smart-mouthed son of a bitch—"

"Don't you call me that!"

Ogren tried to come out fighting. Downey drove his fist into Ogren's stomach and slammed him back against the box car again. He waited until the paralysis left Ogren's body and he could quit choking and retching and fearing death. Downey had caught him smack in the solar plexus, harder than it was safe to hit a man.

"As I was saying," Downey went on, "you smart-mouthed son of a bitch, you had your chance to ride out and you wanted to argue. All right, you just open your mouth or lift your hand to me again—"

Downey slapped him again and again, six times, banging Ogren's head back against the box car with each blow. He unsnapped the flap on Ogren's holster and slipped out the .45, which he stuck in his own pocket. He let Ogren stand alone and wipe away the blood from his split lips.

"Come to the office and get your gun after you've got your horse out to leave town," he said.

He rejoined Louie Varden, happy that he had had this opportunity to demonstrate how he kept order here. Neither man mentioned the incident, but Downey knew it was on Varden's mind. In the courthouse office, Downey kicked a straight-backed chair over to the end of the desk for his guest, and sat down in his own creaking swivel chair behind it.

"Ain't very comfortable, Mr. Varden, but this is a working office." Downey took Ogren's gun out of his pocket and put it in a desk drawer.

"Comfortable for me," replied the railroad dick. "I'm Louie to my friends, by the way."

"Well, Louie, my friends call me Rodge."

"I reckon you know why I'm here, Rodge."

"No idee."

"Chesty Bob Nylander."

Downey felt his every muscle go taut. "Jesus, you don't reckon he's in Hillary County, do you?"

"No reason to think he is, no reason to think he ain't. We have talked to two members of his past gangs, and they tell us—"

"Who is 'we'?"

The bobcat eyes narrowed resentfully. "Some of us who are interested in him. We—"

"Why is the UP interested in him? He never robbed the railroad, did he?"

"You sure brace your feet and pull, don't you? No, he ain't never hit us, that's right. But we're told that he's going to do it soon."

Downey shook his head wonderingly. "Why? What could he steal from a depot? A few hundred dollars, if he was lucky."

"Well . . . more than that, mebbe. But the thing is, this jaybird just figgers he's the greatest robber that ever cantered down the turnpike. His ambition is to outshine the James Boys, Jesse and Frank. He's already better than they was at robbing banks, and all he has to do is rob a train now, to go down in history."

"Rob a *train?* Hell, Louie, that is about as stylish as plowing with oxen. When is he supposed to rob this train, and where?"

"That's what we don't know. But somewhere in Wyoming, and soon. The railroad I have the good fortune to represent is offering a reward of one thousand dollars for him, dead or alive. Now, as a UP employee, I could not ever, in no way, collect on that reward. But there's another twenty-five hundred offered by the banks—"

"Two thousand is all I know about."

"No, the Utah Banking Association has come up with five hundred. The dodgeroos will be in the mail by the end of the week. Now, from what we hear from these two old comrades of Nylander's—"

"Listen, if they know that much about him, why don't they tell you where he is, so you can go out and gather up the crop on the son of a bitch?"

"They don't know where he is. They don't even *want* to know where he is. And they don't want him to know where they are. Chesty Bob Nylander don't think no more of murdering a man than you and I do of swatting a fly. And yet, what strikes me about him is that he can talk men into working with him when they know he aims to kill them afterward!

Now, robbing banks is a chancy trade at best. You tell me why a man will go into it if he knows in advance that his leader is going to kill him for his share of the loot, if there's any way he can do it."

"Why," Downey murmured, "I reckon if you're ignorant enough to be a bank robber, you're so short on brains you figger you're going to be the one to do the killing. And maybe this fella is just some kind of a bossy leader, a born sergeant that people can't help but follow."

"I size him up that way myself."

"How can I help you then, Louie?"

"Why, I wish you and me could go around and talk to a few of your people, and set up a—"

"What people?"

"Why, your banker. Your judge. Your county commissioners. Your leading citizens. I wish we could all work together on this, and I'm authorized to pledge my company's full assistance. If we don't, this fellow is liable to prove that he *is* better than the James Boys."

And you'll be in a position to whack up the reward from the banks. Go up and down the UP, tell the same story to every sheriff in UP territory, and cash in no matter where Chesty Bob hit.

What a comfort to have Chesty Bob living in his own house, under his own eye, in his own town, thinking himself secure in his disguise! A sudden inspiration came to Downey, and he let a look of disappointment fall heavily across his face. He shook his head.

"I'd be glad to accommodate you, Louie, except that me and the wife are leaving for Omaha on tonight's train. She has a grandmother dying in Omaha, don't you see, and I've never took her there in all the time we been married. The truth is, I been married to this damn job, and I can't let her down in this sad time."

Before Varden could reply, the door opened and Monte Barrett came in, leading Chet Wilson by a short length of chain. Wilson's hair had been clipped close to his skull, and he wasn't a bad-looking bird with his face shaved. He reeked of lilacs and wore a big, foolish grin.

"If you'd just find me a nice girl, Sheriff, I'm ready to go buggy-riding," he said.

"Get your ass back in your cell and shut up," Downey said. "Monte, lock him in and then you go dung out the barn."

Varden waited until they were alone again before leaning forward to speak in a low voice. "Wait until tomorrow night, Rodge, and I'll see that you're on the palace car and it won't cost you a cent."

"I dunno, Louie. That's nice of you, but the old lady could be dead by now."

"Rodge, do me this favor. Wire them, my expense, and ask how she is. Send it reply prepaid. We can hear back in three, four hours. You ever been on a palace car? It would be a real treat for Mrs. Downey. It would be a big favor to me and the Union Pacific."

That was what Downey had been waiting to hear—that he would be granting the favor, and under no obligation to anyone. Ten minutes later the depot agent was speeding off a message to Clytie's uncle in Omaha, at the address Downey took from the letter:

HOW IS GRANDMA QUESTION MARK STILL TIME FOR ME TO GET THERE QUESTION MARK PLEASE REPLY AT ONCE PREPAID CARE OF LOUIS VARDEN THIS STATION STOP GIVE HER MY DEAREST LOVE.

The "dearest love" was Varden's idea, and not a bad one. Now Downey had no excuse for not escorting Varden around town to proselyte for vigilance against Chesty Bob. The first person they met was Monte Barrett, who had ripped his pants on a nail in the courthouse barn and was going home to have Lena sew it up.

"Holy smoke! Everybody knows about you, Mr. Varden,"

Monte said reverently when he was introduced. "It sure is an honor to meet you, sir."

(Hey, what the hell is going on here? I never knowed this Varden was so famous. And why is he bothering to snake-charm poor simple Monte?)

"The honor is mine," Varden said in that soft voice of his that made a man prick up his ears to hear at all. He kept pumping Monte's red hand, lingeringly. "We peace officers must all work together, Monte. Hope it's all right to call you that? My name is Louie."

In his most reckless moments Downey had never thought of Monte Barrett as being worth cultivating. Now that he was forced to reconsider, and study Monte all over again, he still did not. This Louie Varden just was not as smart as he was supposed to be, that was all.

CHAPTER 4

It was an uneasy three hours for Rodgerson E. Downey. It seemed to him that he was sitting in about three big games—really big ones, in which he was playing for high stakes, shooting the moon on every bet. The biggest one should have been Chesty Bob Nylander, who represented not just reward money but a victory that could make him lieutenant governor. When a man shoved his whole future into the pot, surely it was the biggest gamble he would ever make.

But Clytie kept coming between Downey and the cards he held in the Chesty Bob game. He supposed he had already lost her, just when he realized how much he wanted her. It was like a knife in his guts to think, What I really want is for Clytie to be happy. . . . For, inevitably, the next thought was always, With that bank-robbing, wig-wearing, son of a bitch of a barber? It ain't possible. . . . He even found himself wishing wildly that the two of them would turn up missing some morning—run off together, eloped, gone for good where no one would ever find them. Take the decision out of his hands, at least.

The third game was plain old survival, when you came right down to it. He had never enjoyed an election campaign, and the moment he had won one he had started dreading the one two years away. If everything crashed, if he let Chesty Bob make a fool of him, and Clytie left him an object of ridicule, how could he even hang on to his job in the election next year?

So it was three hours later when a small boy came, panting, to the Hillary Hotel with word from the depot agent that there was a telegram that Louie Varden had to sign for. Downey had resolutely refused to introduce Varden to anyone until the matter of the tickets was settled. Varden was boiling, that was plain, but let him boil.

The message, addressed to Clytie in care of Varden, said:

DOCTOR SAYS MATTER OF DAYS FOR GRANDMA STOP IT
WOULD DO HER SO MUCH GOOD TO SEE YOU STOP COUSIN
MILTON AILING TOO AND LOTTIES MIDDLE BOY BROKE ARM
STOP I AINT SO PEART MYSELF

BARRINGTON J. TATE

Varden signed for the wire, then handed it to Downey to open. Downey handed it back for Varden to read.

"One more day won't hurt, Rodge," Varden pleaded. "Why don't we get your tickets now, for tomorrow night's train, and then you and me get to work?"

"Round trippers."

"Sure."

"Palace car both ways."

Varden mopped his face with a hand that trembled around his bunched kerchief. "Sure, sure, but then let's go talk to some people. It's important to the UP to fall on this miscreant like a ton of bricks, before he can try a damn-fool train robbery and mebbe kill somebody."

Downey, his spirits rising, studied the famed detective narrowly, seeing only a man who pulled his pants on one leg at a time, the same as everybody else. "And that reward prob'ly means something to you, too," he said.

The veiled hazel eyes dropped briefly. "I told you, Rodge, I can't draw on the UP money. But I'd be free to share in the other rewards."

"What's your idee of a share?"

"Why, altogether now, there's forty-five hundred dollars, twenty-five hundred of it bank money. Now, just suppose we make it a butchering split." Varden laughed hollowly.

"What do you call a butchering split?"

"Each of us takes a half of the hog, and you take the tail and head and liver."

"No, Louie, price it out for me." Downey wanted to mop the nervous sweat from his own face, but swore not to weaken that much. He might never be this much man again, but, while it lasted, he was Varden's master.

"Well, you take the railroad money and five hundred of the bank money, and I take the other two thousand of the bank money."

And what a bargain that was! He'd make the same deal or better with every sheriff along the UP, so no matter who lost, Louie Varden won.

"I reckon not," Downey said.

"Why not?" It was almost a sob.

"Several reasons. First, maybe I got my own idees about where Chesty Bob is—maybe I know more than you do. Second, I'd have to consult with my friends before I made any kind of agreement about anything."

"What friends?"

"Well, you see, I been asked to run for lieutenant governor next year." Downey found himself again riding the bucking horse of inspiration, with no idea of where he was going or how to get off. "I couldn't make no deal like this without their advice."

"You mean Randolph Crocker."

Downey remembered hearing that name, but he had no idea who Randolph Crocker was. He nodded mysteriously and said, "Well, him and a few more."

"I hadn't heard about you running."

"It's still pretty secret, but I know I can trust you." About as far as I could butt this depot with my bare head . . .

Varden was gray-colored, he was so pale. His eyes, wide open for a change, were full of a wildness that made him look to Downey like a plain fool. "Jesus, it sure is a secret! Who else knows, Rodge?"

"That's a secret, too."

"We ain't been asked. If anybody talked to the Union Pacific about it, I'd know."

"Maybe. Maybe not." Downey still bestrode the unbroken horse of inspiration. "But I'll tell you the most important reason of all, Louie, why I can't make any such deal with you. Come here!"

They were standing in the waiting room of the depot, on one wall of which hung a fine, large-scale map of the territory served by the Union Pacific, and contiguous states. In Downey's mind was an orderly catalog of every one of Chesty Bob Nylander's crimes. He had studied the man's record so long and so hard that he felt sure he knew it better than Varden. His thick forefinger tapped out the town names on the map.

"Chesty Bob runs a regular route, like a hardware drummer—Nebraska, then Wyoming, then Kansas, then Colorado. It's a kind of a pattern, see? He never has hit in Utah, and he was last at work in Kansas. His next victim is going to be some bank in Nebraska, and if the UP is hit too, that's where it will be."

"That's not what I hear from his own sidekicks."

"Well, you may be right," Downey said, "and in fact I hope you are, by God. Let that renegade know that I don't stand for no trifling here!"

"All the more reason we should work together, Rodge," Varden said piteously. "Let's go talk to some of your leading citizens, and let me present my company's offer of complete, total, one-hundred-per-cent assistance."

"I really should go give my wife her letter and tell her to get ready for our trip."

"Perfectly reasonable," Varden said in a voice of despair, "and we'll forget today, unless you'll let me stand treat for a dinner at the hotel for you. And we both pitch in tomorrow."

"You're an easy man to work with, Louie."

The UP detective turned over the tickets, and a note to the conductor of Train 2352, to Downey. It was plain that he needed time to think things over. Downey had matched wits with the best in the business, had learned much, and had given away not one shred of his own secret.

But as he plodded up the hill to his house and the meeting with Clytie, his self-confidence flowed away. The house was cold and empty, and his heart broke at the thought that today might have been the day for her and that bank-robbing, wig-wearing fake barber to run away. Then he heard the sound of her hoe, scraping away out in the chicken house. She was never idle, this woman.

He went to the back door. "Clytie! Come in here and let me tell you something. You can do that some other time, woman."

"What other time?" came her reply.

He did not bother to answer. Soon she came through the back door, in her overalls, with a red bandanna over her hair. The overalls had gotten a little tight over her round little bottom, and so had that faded old blouse she wore for a shirt. Clytie wasn't much in the chest, at least with her clothes on. Downey tried to remember what her breasts looked like, and almost choked.

Months ago he had learned to conquer his own desire. It was always such a fight with Clytie, it just wasn't worth it. "Here, read this," he said, and handed her the telegram.

It was the first she had ever received. "Oh! Oh dear, what's this? Is somebody dead?" she wailed.

"Not yet. Take it out and read it, damnit!"

She did so, and then raised a face that was stern and grave, but not woebegone. She shook her head sadly and stared off into a dark corner of the kitchen.

"Poor Grandma! I loved her more than anybody except Mama, and I was always her favorite. She never held it against Papa that he married an Indian."

He ached to take her in his arms and comfort her. He had to clear his throat to speak. "It's too bad. We all have to go, but a person hates to think of a nice old grandma dying."

"It's nothing to you. I'm sorry you was put to such trouble. I know about how much my goddamn family means to you."

"I brung these, too."

He handed her the tickets. Either she did not know what they were or she simply could not believe her eyes. She went still as the granite statue of the Union soldier in the courthouse square. Even when he touched her bare arm with his fingertips she did not move.

"I know you liked your grandma, Clytie," he said. "I thought I'd take a week off, and we'd go there on the train tomorrow night, so you can see her. Your uncle ain't well, either, he says."

"Uncle Barrington was born too ailing to work. You never heard me say I missed him."

"Clytie, don't go back there to quarrel over a death-bed. Don't you want to go? The both of us, I mean. If you was her favorite, your—your *husband*"—he had to force out the word —"ort to be at the death-bed, too."

"Oh, oh, oh! Oh, Rodge, oh, Rodge!"

She crumpled telegram and tickets in her hand, fell against him, and cried noisily. He put an arm around her and patted the small of her back awkwardly. He yearned to take a handful of the shapely little haunch under those tight overalls, but he knew better.

It took her a long time to cry it out, and then she could not face him. She fell into a chair, leaned her chin in her hand on the kitchen table, and looked about at the third button on his shirt.

"I just don't know what to say, Rodge. I never been on a train before."

"Ain't you?"

"No. You have to sleep setting up, like in a chair, don't you?"

"Well, no. This is a palace car, and the chairs are real soft, and covered with plush and velvet, and they lean back to make a bed. The train crew brings you around pillows, and if you need blankets they bring them, too. I never rode in a palace car, but I been in one."

"I want to cry, I been so mean to you."

"There's no time for crying, Clytie. You'll have to pack a suitcase for us, and make some lunch to take along."

"Oh, God, I can't go. I haven't got a dress, I haven't got shoes, I haven't got anything."

Downey winced. "Go down to Sontag's and get what you need. There's time to run up a dress if you start now, ain't there? And stockings—you'll need them. A hat, too, but you can get that in Omaha."

She stood up again, swaying on rubbery legs. "Honest, Rodge, can I buy all that stuff?"

"Tell Erik to charge it. Everything you need."

"Oh, oh, oh! I'll ask Mrs. Sontag to rent me her sewing machine." For a moment he thought she was going to come into his arms again. "Rodge, if I live to be a hundred, I'll never understand you," she said; and turned her back to run into their bedroom.

He personally arranged for the Anderson kids to take care of the chickens, gather the eggs, milk the cow, and pour milk for the Sontag kids to pick up. The Andersons would get the milk and eggs during their absence and the kids would get a nickel a day. He could have asked it as a favor, and Anderson would have been glad to oblige.

But he was through asking for cheap favors. A man who aspired to the second-highest office in the state had to live up to it. All the rest of the afternoon he was buoyed by ambition, inspiration, and the excitement of the coming trip in the palace car. It was not until he came home late that night that the old ticks and lice and unidentified creeping bugs of shame and humility swarmed over him. He had eaten a bad dinner in the hotel, sparring with Varden and winning, but worrying about Clytie and Charley Noble. What a relief to see Charley still in the De Luxe, cutting hair a mile a minute, when finally he could break away from Varden.

But then the bedroom door was closed at home, and when he knocked, Clytie cried, with her mouth full of pins, "Not yet, not yet! It ain't even basted." He slunk up the narrow steps to the attic, where, thank God, he was too tired to lie awake and worry.

● ● ●

Judge Roy Dilham's wife was ill, and he had not been at the courthouse for a week. They found him the next morning, a small man who had once been plump but who now was a handful—an active, wiry handful—of bones. Downey had never felt comfortable around him, having taken his oath of office before the judge. He would never forget the long lecture Dilham had given him, in which he had said, in part:

"Self-government is a burden, and its weight is not shared equally. No, sometimes the President bears a lighter load than the obscure man elected by obscure citizens to do one small job. You are alone now, Sheriff Downey, and always you will be outlined against the blazing sunrise of the future, a target for posterity's complaints. The people's approval is not enough. You must also live with your own soul, and with souls yet unborn."

And so on. The judge was raking dead leaves and weeds out of his dead grass. His wife, covered with an old quilt, lay in a hammock nearby. Downey introduced Varden, and was a little shamed by the detective's oiliness.

"I applaud your zeal," the judge said, "but I don't see what you expect of me."

"Judge, this is a mobilization of righteousness against the worst gang of murdering robbers in the history of our nation. My company, which I compare to a vital vein in the body politic, stands ready to support your people, but there must be local leadership," said Varden.

"The churches are the place to mobilize the forces of righteousness. I can't very well threaten a man who may appear in my court for trial someday."

"Your Honor—"

"We are not in court, Mr. Varden. You embarrass all of us by excessive formality."

"Then I'll speak bluntly. This is no time for legal hair-splitting! The community leadership must be stirred to action!"

"No, the courts must stand aloof. You're talking about political leadership, sir, and there's no shrewder man in that area than Sheriff Downey."

Downey almost rocked on his feet. "That is your honest opinion?" Varden said, almost gurgling.

"Yes. When I first knew Rodgerson Downey, he was a cow-crew boss. Now look at him, head of the best and least-expensive sheriff's office in Wyoming!"

Downey found his voice to choke, "By God, Judge, I never knowed you felt that way, and it sure is a relief to hear it."

"I don't like everything you do, Mr. Downey—but then I don't imagine you endorse everything that I do." Judge Dilham looked back at Varden. "Rodge is a stern man, but not a brutal one. He has few friends, but many, many supporters. And that is the essence of successful political leadership. It's your friends who get you into trouble, Mr. Varden."

"All I do," Downey said quiveringly, "is try to be a sheriff for all the people."

They could get no more out of Judge Dilham, nor did Downey want anything more. It was clear to him that Varden had been more shocked and surprised than Downey himself had been at the judge's praise. Through Downey's agitated mind there suddenly flitted dim faces out of the shameful past. Oh, if *they* could only hear the county judge talking about Rodgerson Downey like that!

They headed for the bank. A man was playing a fiddle in front of the Hillary Hotel, his wide-brimmed hat upside down on the sidewalk beside him. There were a few dimes, many pennies, a nickel or two, and two quarters in it. He was a tall, gaunt man with a big Adam's apple and a big nose, clean-shaven except for a stiff little mustache just going gray. He was dressed in worn but clean range clothing.

They stopped for a moment to listen. Varden dropped two dimes into the hat. "Thank you, kind sir," the fiddler said.

"You play good," said Varden.

"How about you, Mr. Sheriff? Can I persuade you to fee the fiddler, as we all must do eventually?"

"I just wonder," Downey said, "if you have any idee who owns that horse there." He pointed to a fine brown gelding wearing a 51 brand, tied in front of the bank. Saddle and bridle were plain but good. The saddle pouches that hung from the horse's withers, and the leather-covered bedroll behind, bespoke an owner thrifty but proud.

"I do. You want to see my bill of sale?" said the fiddler.

"If I didn't, I wouldn't ask."

The fiddler went to the saddle pouches and, from one, took out a packet of papers wrapped in oilskin. He selected one and handed it to Downey. The document had not merely been signed, it had been notarized in Otoe County, Nebraska. It recited the horse's ownership from birth on the 51 ranch in Richardson County, through four owners, to the present one, Francis E. Feathers. According to the dates on it, the horse should have been seven years old.

Downey returned the bill of sale to the fiddler and went to the horse's head. He persuaded it, expertly, to open its mouth for a quick look at its teeth.

"Seven. He's your horse, Mr. Feathers. You'll understand why I clear up these little things when I tell you that your horse is safe here now. Nobody's going to trifle with him. Anybody does, tell him to see me."

"Thank you kindly, Sheriff. Anybody'll tell you that Fiddler Feathers never done a crooked thing in his life."

They plodded on toward the bank, and Downey had the distinct impression that the incident with the fiddler and his horse had impressed Varden even more than the judge's praise.

Benjamin Chase was the president of the Hillary State Bank and the son of its founder. Downey did not like Ben very well, but it was his hunch that Ben would be good at anything he attempted. He was no more than forty, a brusque, short-spoken, impatient man who was probably burning up with ambition inside.

"What is it you want to know?" he asked after Downey had presented Varden.

"How much cash do you keep in your vaults? What is your practice in shipping specie, both in and out? Are there any big payrolls to be met around here, and what are the payday dates? In short, when will this bank be full of money—when will you be shipping or receiving cash by rail—when would it be a good time for a smart gang of bank robbers to hit you?" Varden recited.

"Anytime." Ben opened his desk drawer and took out a .45, just long enough to let the detective see it. "Three of us have forty-fives. We can all shoot them, and we take target practice regularly. My safe has a triple lock that is made in England—the best, and unfamiliar to most burglars and robbers here. Anytime they want to try to rob us, we're ready."

"For Chesty Bob Nylander, for instance?"

The banker hesitated for a moment. "Him too."

Varden looked at Downey, a look that said, No use talking to this mule-head. They stood up and Downey said, "Try not to shoot your own foot off, Ben, if you get held up. No, now—won't do you no good to get huffy! By the time a robber gang gets inside here, the smartest thing you can do is stand and deliver. If you want to get yourself shot up, go ahead. But I'd hate for you to get some poor bastard that works here killed, for no good reason."

CHAPTER 5

Downey was a nervous wreck by late afternoon. His only consolation was his feeling that he did not show it, while the strain was obviously telling on Louie Varden. The detective insisted on talking to everyone. He did his best to raise panic, and when it failed, when men refused to take fright, he blamed Downey.

And in this he was quite right, and Downey knew it. Not once did he volunteer an opinion contrary to Varden's. He waited until he was asked, and he never said anything more critical than "Mr. Varden prob'ly knows more about it than I do. Us country sheriffs don't get told all the secrets, you know." There was nothing Varden could do but choke down his resentment and smile, smile, smile.

The last man they talked to was Hugh Dean, a stroke of luck because Dean merely happened to be in town. The owner of the HD was the closest thing Downey had to a friend. Hugh was close to seventy, Downey knew, but he looked fifty-five. He had survived three wives, each of whom had given him three children. He would leave each child comfortably fixed when he died. The males were all hard workers, the females married to hard workers. It had always seemed to Downey that the Deans constituted a human stud-farm that would be a credit to Wyoming for generations to come.

Varden seemed to know that he was talking to someone who counted. "Glad I got this chance to talk to you, sir," he said oilily. "I don't seem to make no headway with Rodge, here, since he's so excited about starting up his campaign for lieutenant governor."

Downey wished he could die, but old Hugh did not even look around at him. "Rodge don't need to worry about no campaign," he said. "His friends will take care of it."

"Yes. Yes. What I'm interested in, of course, is catching Chesty Bob Nylander before he can rob the Union Pacific and some bank loaded with more cash than it should be carrying."

"Best way to see that it don't happen is, when there's a money train due, keep it a secret. I declare, you might as well take an ad in the papers!"

Downey pricked up his ears at the unfamiliar term "money train." Varden turned green. "We try to keep it confidential," he said, "but when you've got to take local banks into your confidence by mail, you're trusting too many people."

"Why not by wire, then?"

"It costs a lot, for one thing."

"Not as much as a robbery would."

"Yes, but anybody can get to the wires, because every depot agent knows what comes over them."

"Oh, shoot! Do it in code. Get yourself a bunch of code words to represent the numbers, one to fifteen. Each month, you mail out a sealed list of that month's code words to the bankers. They don't open them until they get the wire, see? Let's say that 'purple' means 'one' and 'shoe-horn' means 'nine' and 'bucket' means thirteen, and so on," Hugh said.

"Your banker gets a wire from some made-up name he don't know, and the wire don't say a damn thing. Just 'Silver souvenir shoe-horn lost advise if found.' Well then, Mr. Banker opens his code list up and sees that 'shoe-horn' means 'nine.' He tears up the wire and the code list and gets ready for a money train nine days from today. He don't mark his calendar, or tell even his own wife, see.

"But he's ready, and the risk is over for him in a matter of minutes—and the railroad, too. The train is in Cheyenne or Omaha before anybody can talk."

"Genius, pure genius!" said Varden. "It would take some organization, though."

"Rodge Downey is the best man at running some kind of organization that I know of."

"But he don't take Chesty Bob very serious."

"Just because he don't run around like a chicken with its head off, don't you bet he don't know what's going on. In fact, I'd be willing to bet he knows as much about Chesty Bob as you do, and maybe more."

The interview was over, as far as Hugh Dean was concerned. Downey and Varden departed, the sheriff itching to get home and make sure Clytie was prepared for the trip.

"If you know something about Chesty Bob that you ain't told me," Varden said, "you might show your goodwill by being frank, Rodge."

"Yes, I might," said Downey, "and you might tell me what the hell a money train is, too. Why do I have to find out things like this from my own people?"

"I ain't supposed to tell nobody."

"Then don't. I'll find out."

Varden whimpered, "These county-seat banks are always getting in more cash than they like to keep on hand, or running short of it when they need it, and it's up to us to transport it safely. Actually, it's up to the express companies, but you know who gets blamed if a train is robbed and the express car is dynamited. We tried to set up a plan where one day a month we'd carry four or five detectives to help guard the express car. So fur, we never been robbed. But goddamn if it don't seem to me that people along the line know more about it than I do. Why, the little kids stand along the track to watch the money train go by, the way these bankers blab, blab, blab."

"You sure don't do any blabbing, though. I have to look like a jackass in front of my own people. I'll buy you a beer, Louie, and then I got to go up and help my wife get ready for her sad journey."

They stepped into the Elkhorn saloon, billiard parlor, and card room. Just as Downey was lifting his glass in a salute to Varden, his heart almost stopped pumping. There, across the room, leaning against the wall and watching a card game, was the man himself. The one and only Chesty Bob Nylander, *alias* Charley Noble.

Charley looked up and saw them. He got that big, silly, yokel smile under his silly steerhorn mustache and came over to them. "Clytie tells me I'm going to be a bachelor for a few days, Mr. Downey. It's too bad about her grandma, but I hope you have nice trip," he said.

There was nothing to do but introduce them. Varden was unhappy and absent-minded. Downey would have bet that he was bitterly regretting having stood treat for two round-trip parlor-car tickets to Omaha. His smile was stiff when he offered his hand in farewell.

"I hope you don't figger you wasted your time here, Louie," Downey said.

"Not at all. Pleasure to meet a sheriff with the popularity you got. I do hope, though, that you'll be giving that matter a lot of careful thought."

"You can count on that, Louie. And you think about that other idee about the code, too."

"Oh, I will, Rodge, you bet I will."

"If you're going home now, Rodge," Charley said, "I'll walk along with you."

"I've got to get my horse out of the courthouse stable. I don't want to leave him there for Monte to neglect. I hope you'll see to my horses while I'm gone."

"I'll take care of them like they's my own, and I'll walk over with you and get the one from the courthouse now."

There was no getting rid of him. By the time they reached home, Clytie had finished her milking and her other outside chores and was putting supper on the table. "Ain't nothing but fried eggs and fried potatoes and some sausage," she apologized. "I meant to kill a hen, but I been *so* busy."

The sausage fried down at last winter's butchering was long gone. "Where'd you get sausage?" Downey asked.

"From the store. It's fresh-ground."

"And dear, too, I bet."

"Everything a Sontag touches turns to gold. She charged me twenty cents to use her sewing machine and ten cents for breaking an old bent needle that was in it."

"Your dress done?"

"One is. I made two. A body wants to look her best for a train trip."

"You'll be all smoked up from the engine."

"Really? Oh, Rodge, I can't wait. I can't, I can't! It seems like a dream that can't come true."

He started toward her unthinkingly, his arms ready to enclose her. She skipped aside, saying something about killing some chickens to fry for their lunch on the train. Not until Charley Noble spoke did Downey remember that the son of a bitch was standing there gawking.

"I'll kill the chickens for you," Charley said. "How many? Mr. Downey will be wanting a bath. The water's hot. Why don't you go on down and have one, Mr. Downey?"

And leave you alone with Clytie? I reckon not. . . .

"Just get out of my way, both of you," Clytie cried wildly. "Go get your bath, Rodge. And let him shave you up, too."

Silently the two men plodded back down the hill to the shop, Downey carrying his clean clothing under his arm. When they came out of the shop he was amazed at how late it was, how swiftly darkness was falling. Then a soft but sharp breath of cold air slid past him, and his weather-wise nerves reacted instantaneously.

"We're in for a storm! It's going to blow like hell here in a minute," he exclaimed.

Charley tugged at his mustache, staring admiringly at him. "I declare, how do you know that, Mr. Downey?"

"Any fool knows that an east wind this time of year means

a storm. Go tell Clytie to lock up. I'll see to the courthouse and be up as soon as I can."

At night, Miller Mahaffey used Downey's office as his headquarters. Miller had lost a leg at Antietam and drew ten dollars a month pension. He slept above the livery stable and earned another ten a month there. He mopped out the Elkhorn twice a week for still another ten. A fourth ten came from his stipend as Hillary town constable.

Miller was in Downey's chair, reading, with his spectacles down on the end of his nose. "Your prisoner is complaining about being locked up tonight, Rodge. Claims there's a cyclone coming," he said.

"You tell him my jurisdiction don't cover cyclones." Downey gave a jerk of his head, and Miller got his wooden leg under him and followed him outside as silently as he could. "It's late in the season for a cyclone, Miller," Downey whispered, "but we could have one, so you keep a sharp eye out. If one comes, turn the prisoner loose."

"Well, if you say so. But what's Judge Dilham going to think about it?"

"That ain't your worry. If he don't want my prisoner killed, let him put out an injunction against the cyclone." He offered Miller his hand. "Take care of things, and try to help that damn fool of a Monte Barrett from making too many mistakes."

"I will, Rodge. Have a good trip."

"Ain't so sure it's safe to leave in a storm."

He became less and less sure as he hurried up the hill to the house. Clytie was stitching away at one of her dresses, by lamplight. Two big skillets filled with frying chickens crackled away on the stove. On impulse, Downey put his face down between Clytie and her sewing.

"What's the matter with you? I'm trying to finish, can't you see?" she snapped.

"Smell me. Witch hazel and bay rum!"

"You smell like a Cheyenne sporting house."

His heart fell. He was halfway across the room before he thought to say, "How do you know what a Cheyenne sporting house smells like?"

"Go pack your clothes and let a body be. You got clean socks and a clean shirt, and I bought you some new underwear."

The wind was driving leaves and small brush in eddying currents across the back yard. From somewhere higher up the hill, where the wind was stronger, he heard the crash of a limb breaking off of a naked tree.

"I dunno, Clytie. The weather scares me."

"*You*, scared of the weather? You?"

"I think mebbe we ought to put this trip off."

"Oh, no! No, we can't do that," she wailed.

Her face broke his heart, yet at the same time he yearned to slap it. "Let me take another look. You pack my duds for me. But by God, woman, I ain't going away and leaving this town to a cyclone!"

"What could you do to stop a cyclone?"

She would be the death of him, with that mind she had. He went out and down the hill, hearing more tree limbs breaking as he leaned into the strong wind. As a scared kid, even up into his twenties, he had always feared storms—all kinds, high wind, high water, lightning. In the last few years, since becoming sheriff, all these fears had left him, somehow. It was even a pleasure to walk in a storm, even tonight.

A couple of store windows had been broken, but there was no serious damage that he could see. He stood alone on a corner for a long time, eyes cocked skyward, ears groping for tiny sounds. It came to him that it was going to blow itself out. The peak winds had already passed. There would be no rain, and when this was all over it would probably turn cold.

He returned to the house and there, in the kitchen, Clytie and Charley were gabbling away like grave-robbers. Clytie was still sewing on her dress. Charley was chomping on a plate of fried chicken and drinking a big glass of fresh buttermilk.

"What the hell's going on here?" he growled.

"What do you think is going on?" Clytie retorted. "That old cottonwood limb blowed down across the calf pen. Charley took the lantern and made sure the calf was all right, and patched up the fence."

"I don't think it's going to amount to nothing, Mr. Downey," Charley said around a mouthful of chicken. "I hope we get some rain, though. The range needs it."

"I hope that chicken is tasty," Downey said.

"It sure is. Your wife can fry chicken fine."

"I hope there's a little left to take on the train with us."

"Yes, sir. My feeling is that this storm is over."

Downey almost said, "And my feeling is that you're making mighty free with my house and my wife and my fried chicken," but he held it back. Charley belched, wiped his mouth delicately on his sleeve, and tweaked his mustache back into shape. He went out back to the privy and came back yawning.

"I told you it wouldn't amount to a hill of beans. It has plumb stopped blowing. Goodnight," he said, and went into his room in the lean-to off the kitchen.

"Goodnight, Charley. I reckon we won't see you until we get back from our trip," Clytie said.

Downey said nothing. The door closed. Clytie stood up. "I'll go pack the last things. I reckon it's about time."

"I reckon."

"Oh, Rodge, ain't you excited?"

He grunted. He did not look around as she headed toward the bedroom. When she trailed the tips of her fingers through his hair, he was so startled—shocked, really—that he sat there like a stone for a moment. Then it took real courage to get up and follow her into the bedroom and close the door behind him.

She was in the act of pulling her old house dress off over her head. She was in camisole and a pair of pantalettes that he had never seen before, a thin material with three little ruffles at the bottom of each leg and a pink drawstring ribbon at the top. She looked cute as a colt in her underwear, especially turning as pink as she suddenly was.

"What I want to know," he said in a low voice, "is why I have to take a bath to go on a train trip, and you don't."

"I had mine this afternoon, in the kitchen." She held up her arms and spun around for him. "How do you like my pants and cammie, Rodge? I bought them out of my egg money. I—I never had anything like this before."

He reached for her. She retreated, laughing, eyes bright in a rosy face, like the Clytie of years ago. He trapped her against the wall, and reached behind her to take a handful of her firm little bottom.

"Go 'long, now. No time for foolishness," she whispered, struggling with both hands at his wrist.

Resistance only inflamed him more. He crushed her to him, tilted her head back, and made her kiss him. She kissed him back once, and then again, and then she had had enough. She twisted her face out of the way.

"Save some of that for a strange bed, why don't you?" she giggled. "Don't spoil it now, Rodge. Let's make this a honeymoon," was all she said.

He could have cried, he felt so happy. He went out because that was what she wanted, and waited until she opened the door and told him to come get the valises. He felt a strange sadness to see her in a new dress, wearing new shoes with mother-of-pearl buttons, with her hair piled in a mountain of braids on top of her head.

"You are a goddamn good-looking woman, Clytie," he said. He got out his hand-tooled holster and belt, with the pearl-handled .45 that Hugh Dean had given him after his first election. He put on his wide-brimmed black hat and clawhammer coat. I bet I look like a goddamn Reb Democrat politician, he thought, remembering back to the days of his youth.

● ● ●

The eastbound Flyer was ten minutes late, having slowed down for the high winds. Louie Varden was there to see them off, with a courtly bow for Clytie and a look of surprise for Downey. The conductor bustled about, showing them elaborate consideration. He had saved two fine seats in the palace car, he said.

Others had heard about the trip, and Downey had several hands to shake before he could board the train. The conductor moved ahead, escorting them to their seats. Downey had to take Clytie's elbow, so stricken was she by the grandeur of the car. It was truly magnificent, mahogany hardwood, seats upholstered in a deep, figured plush of a rich blue, lamps with roses and goddesses and birds on their chimneys. The conductor bowed and extended a hand, palm upward.

"Here you are, reserved for the sheriff and his lady. I'll have the porter bring you pillows and blankets, and there's a box of chocolate cremes for the lady."

He had to put Clytie into the window seat like a helpless child. The nearest lamp had a rose-colored chimney, and in its light she was about the prettiest thing he had ever seen. She wriggled her lithe body against the plush and then leaned against him when he sat down.

"Oh my stars, Rodge, ain't it beautiful?" she sighed, clenching her hands together on the rosewood arm of the seat between them.

He dropped his right hand over both of hers. "Not a bit too good for you, woman," he whispered. "Ort to take a trip like this every now and then."

"I never dreamed of anything so wonderful." Her voice broke into a soft sob. She had to lower her face against his sleeve to hide the tears. "Oh, Rodge, we'll have a good time together, won't we? I—I'll make it up to you, I promise I will."

Desire shook him hard as he realized what she meant. The train started, and Clytie whimpered with excruciating excitement. And then the damned conductor was standing there, rubbing his hands together.

"The dining car is two cars ahead. Most folks has already et, but they got steak, buffalo tongue, ham, turkey, and trout left."

Shyness, not frugality, made them decline. Downey filled their folding cups with ice water from the tanks in the end of the car, and they dined on fried chicken and buttered fresh bread. Suddenly a porter appeared, bearing a tray with a jug of hot coffee, sugar, cream, and cups with the UP crest and President Lincoln's wreathed portrait.

"Compliments of the line, seh. Would you and Madam prefer apple pie, mince pie, raisin pie, or Vienna chocolate-and-rum cake?"

They opted recklessly for cake. Clytie wept as she ate hers. "Oh, God, it's so perfect I want to die. I don't deserve it, Rodge, I been such a bitch."

He patted her arm. "There, now," he whispered. "'Tain't a bit too good for my Clytie."

CHAPTER 6

Clytie was dying to go to the toilet but could not bear to make herself conspicuous by going alone, nor ask him to help her find it. The train pounded through the mountains. Before midnight it stopped briefly at a small cluster of twinkles that meant a sleeping town. Most of the people in the palace car were asleep, but two or three got off here, and two or three more got on.

While there were other people on their feet, Clytie decided to risk finding the toilet marked "Ladies." Downey, however, remembered the sign in the "Gents": *Do Not Flush While Standing in the Station,* and he supposed it was the same in the other one. He whispered a warning to her. She lost heart and sat down.

Soon after the train started moving again a man came plodding down the aisle, searching the faces of the passengers. He was a plump, well-dressed, kindly looking old man with white side-whiskers. He looked them over carefully before pausing there.

"I hope I have the honor of addressing Sheriff Rodgerson E. Downey?" he said, with a courtly nod to Clytie.

"That's me."

"I heard you were aboard. My name is Randolph Crocker. May I sit down?"

The governor's right-hand man! Crocker did something or other to the aisle seat in front of Downey, and the whole back slid forward, to make a seat facing backward. He sat down, saying, "And this, I presume, is Mrs. Downey? I have heard so much of her beauty and grace, and I'm so glad to meet you. So very glad, Mrs. Downey!"

He reached for her hand. Poor, suffering Clytie had to give it to him. He folded it between his and gazed smilingly into her eyes, and Downey realized that there was nothing kindly about him. Louie Varden had been busy on the telegraph again, catching Crocker on one of his prowling political trips to the West.

That undertaker's smile suddenly took the heart out of Downey. This was the one thing he had never been able to cope with—that is, the sublime gall of a thief and liar who meant to do you in and who smiled right into your eyes as he did it. Externally, Downey was still the sheriff of all the people, but inside he was fearful and unsure of himself, and filled with the vague shame that had oppressed him through all his young manhood.

"I'll keep your husband awake only a moment or two, madam." Crocker brought his fishy gaze back to Downey. "What's this I hear about you thinking you might make the race for lieutenant governor?"

His own queasy inner uncertainty made Downey gruffer than he felt was safe with this man. "Who says I'm thinking that?"

"Well, I hear things, you know."

"From Louie Varden."

"Among others. Is it true?"

"No!"

Crocker, startled, batted his eyes. "But I heard that you were seriously thinking of—"

Downey took the plunge out of sheer fury and terror, cutting in to say, "You heard wrong, then. Some of my friends was thinking about it. They got up a little meeting and voted to ask me to run. I said I'd think about it."

"But you just said that you weren't."

"I'm not. I done made up my mind. I'm going to run."

There, it was out, and Downey thought he was going to throw up all over his own lap.

"I wonder if you would step down to the smoking car with me to discuss this further?" Crocker said, when he had his breath back.

"No need," Clytie said coldly, standing up. "Beg you to excuse me, please."

Both got up, and she went toward the rear of the car, Downey having told her that he had found "Gents" at the front end when he went for ice water. Crocker's eyes followed her with frank admiration.

"Lovely woman—lovely, lovely!" he murmured. "Such carriage, such style, so patrician!"

He had hit upon a word that Downey knew, having listened to Judge Dilham talk about the conflict between the patricians and the plebeians in ancient Rome. But Clytie? Patrician, for Christ's sake? Downey wished he could see her, but his back was to her.

"You know," Crocker said, "this isn't the way we do things, Sheriff Downey."

"What ain't?"

"Why, the party has been successful by remaining a party, not just a bunch of ambitious—"

"The way *I* do things ain't always the way *we* do things. I can beat the ass off of anybody you put up, Mr. Crocker. Especially a lawyer. What the hell kind of folks do you think we've got in Wyoming, that would vote for a lawyer over an honest, fighting sheriff?"

"Nobody knows you, Mr. Downey. I hate to be contentious, but really, outside your own county, nobody knows you."

"They soon will."

"Why?"

Downey merely shook his head and looked away. Crocker took out a cigar, fingered it, stared at it, and started to put it in his mouth. Then he remembered where he was and put it back in his pocket. He looked up at Downey.

"I don't know how we came so close to downright disagreement," he said, with that smile that made Downey think he could smell the embalming fluid. "Of course, we may find you're exactly the candidate we want, but you ought to give us a chance to think it over. In fact—and I say this with due concern for the fact that it's generally known that the governor consults with me—in fact, I like the idea of you running better and better."

"Good!"

"But you don't want to run as a lone wolf. Say—!"

Obviously a startling idea had just come to Crocker, but Clytie had returned and they had to rise and let her into her seat. Downey surmised from her relaxed face that she had been successful, but something about her eyes made him uneasy.

"Say what?" he said when they were seated again.

"You know, there are some deputy-marshals' jobs opening up in Arizona and New Mexico. I was discussing them with the attorney general in Washington just a couple of weeks ago. You know, Sheriff Downey, I'm almost sure I could offer you one of them. I know I can, in fact."

"I don't think so, Randy; in fact, I'm just not interested," Downey said easily, and he could almost feel Clytie relax.

"Those are good jobs." When Downey did not reply, Crocker went on, with just a touch of impatience, "You're on your way to Cheyenne, I reckon. I'm getting out at the next junction, little duty call I've got to make to an aged aunt, but I'll give you my card with a note on it, and you stop in and shake hands with the governor."

He took a stub pencil from his pocket and a card from his card case. Downey said, "I won't be stopping in Cheyenne at all. We're going straight on to Omaha. In fact, we don't even change trains at the North Platte division point. This car goes right on through."

Crocker went right on writing. "Maybe you can stop when you come through on the way back."

"We'll sure try, but I ain't sure," Downey said, pocketing the card without reading it.

Crocker stood up and offered his hand. Downey had to rise to take it. "Sheriff," said Crocker, "I'm interested in how you expect to become better known in the state."

"I just don't see how I can keep from it, and that's about all I can say now."

Crocker had gotten a little stiff, but he was back in command of himself now. His hand clasp was strong, his smile wider and more insincere than ever. "Not much opportunity for a sheriff to distinguish himself. Of course, you run an economical office—we're all aware of that, indeed we are—and a very fine one. But for most men it's a blind alley, unless you capture somebody like this Chesty Bob Nylander."

"Well, I might have to do that, too."

"Do you mean that?"

"I don't mean nothing special about it."

"Hm, very interesting! We'll watch and see what develops. Thank you so much for this little chat—thanks to your gracious and lovely wife for tolerating me. I tell you, Sheriff, half the battle of politics is a wife like yours. But you know that, of course."

He smiled his meretricious farewell and went on down the aisle and out of the palace car.

"Well!" said Clytie.

"Well what?" said Downey.

"Who is that bum?"

"Just the most important politician in the state, is all."

"What's he talking about, you running for lieutenant governor?"

"He ain't the only one talking about it."

"You?"

Her incredulity angered him. He turned angrily. "Why is it so funny? I won plenty of elections. Lieutenant governor is a nothing job. They usually get some old poop that's too old to get up in time to do a day's work. I could win that election."

"Does Hugh Dean know about this?"

"Yes. He's all for it."

"Jeeminy!" She was silent, thinking it over. Humble and shy and green Clytie might be, but he awaited her opinion with shortened breath and fist-clenched anxiety. "Maybe so. But listen, Rodge—don't have anything to do with that Crocker."

"Why not?"

"Why, you can tell just by looking at him that he's slippery as two eels screwing in a barrel of snot."

"I don't have to take his deal. He has to take mine, him and the goddamn governor both."

Another moment of silence. Then Clytie said, "Is that really why we took this trip? You didn't mean to have a honeymoon with me at all! You're just campaigning for yourself, like you always do. Everything you do is always for yourself!"

"Clytie, for the Lord's sake, how was I going to know this jaybird was on the train? I swear an oath that I was as surprised as you was," he said, holding up his right hand.

"I hope so."

"That's a hell of a thing to say, after I swore an oath. 'I hope so'!"

"Well, you never done anything nice for me before. You don't treat me like a wife. You treat me like some Indian squaw, too tight to spend a dime on me, you don't even talk to me, you'd rather be in your damn office or the pool hall than home with me—"

He could not hold it in. "Maybe," he said, "if you acted more like a wife, it'd be easier. You won't go out and campaign with me, even when I offered to buy a buggy. You won't go to picnics. I can't have people up to the house for supper like other men, because you slop around in your goddamn bare feet and set there scowling like a damn squaw with a boil on your butt. If I'm sheriff, if we own a house and some land and our own livestock, it sure as hell ain't because you got out and helped me get elected. Your no-good brothers, *they'll* get out and campaign for me, *they* don't think it's a disgrace; why, I bet if I wrote to them that I was running for lieutenant governor, they'd quit their jobs and come back and— But what's the use of talking to you? '*And be sure and bring Clytie out to spend a day sometime,*'" he said mincingly. "How often do you think I've heard that? What the hell do I tell them, Clytie? That you're too goddamn good to associate with the people that vote for me? But it's no use talking about it. Could you even get off your rump to take Judge Dilham's wife a pot of soup when she's been sick? Oh no, not you, not Clytie . . ."

He strangled on his own fury, and the strange thing was that he had never before really been aware of all these shortcomings in her. He had taken it for granted that campaigning was a man's job, and that Clytie fulfilled her function by attesting him a married man. Where, he thought, did we go wrong? She never has been sociable, but . . .

She had run her arm through his and was pressing her face against his. He could feel her body shake with sobs that she tried to keep silent. Instinct told him to remain silent, but not stiff. He relaxed, and let her feel it. In a moment he put his hand on one of hers.

"Oh, Rodge, I told you I been a bitch! If you'd only asked me! I thought you never *wanted* me to. And I wouldn't blame you. The Tates was—the Tates is—you know what a deadbeat Daddy was."

"All I know about the Tates," he whispered, "is that if there was a job anywhere, a Tate had it, and if you had a horse down or hay to get in before a rain or somebody sick, the place would be swarming with your brothers and sisters before you could say Jack Robinson. That's why I never could figger you out. You wouldn't help me."

"You didn't ever say you wanted me to."

"I'm saying it now. Does that satisfy you?"

"Oh yes, Rodge."

She calmed herself before the conductor himself, not a porter, brought pillows and soft woolen blankets. Clytie, exhausted or perhaps just at peace with herself, could not keep her eyes open. Downey figured out how to make the seat recline. He put the pillow under her head and tucked the blanket in around her, and stood up to turn down the rose-colored lamp.

Already she was asleep. He stood there for a moment, studying this half-Indian wife of his—or quarter-Indian, whichever the hell it was. Now that he could back off and size her up, in new clothes, and with her hair fixed, she was really a pretty woman. A lot prettier than when they had gotten married. It struck him that, had she not been his wife, here was the kind of woman he could lust after.

But patrician? Suddenly, out of his youth and young manhood came a ghost, a flock of ghosts, making the word a pressure of bile in his throat. In his mind, he drew his pearl-handled .45 on them, saying, All right, you high-born sons of bitches, fan your tails out of my county or I'll leak some of that blue blood out of you. I'm a disgrace, am I? I'm an ingrate, am I? I'll tell you what I am, by God I'm the sheriff, the sheriff, the sheriff, I'm the sheriff of this county, that's what I am. . . .

The train made the briefest of stops. Downey stood up to look out the window, and saw Randolph Crocker walking toward a waiting buckboard, carrying his bag. The train was in motion immediately. Clytie did not stir, nor did she awaken at the two or three other stops they made before daylight began to seep through the grimy window. But Downey remained wide awake, nervous, indecisive.

He had not made up his mind when the train began to slow down for Curtin. It was an older, greener, tamer town than Hillary. It was also closer to Cheyenne and the sources of power. Downey sat rigidly erect, his throat knotted in a spasm, as the first houses slid past in the cold, gray light of dawn.

The change in speed, the soft clanking under the car as the brakes took hold, awakened Clytie. Her arms came out from under the blanket.

"Where are we?" she murmured.

He could not answer. He knew that he had to make his escape, but for the moment he was paralyzed by moral cowardice. Clytie sat up, yawning and fumbling with the heavy braids that were coiled on top of her head.

"What's the matter, Rodge? You've got such a funny look on your face."

Outside, the conductor called, "All abo-o-o-oard!" Downey heard the thump of the boarding stool being tossed to the steel platform of the vestibule. His neck seemed to creak as he turned toward the window.

"By God, I know that man! He's wanted! Oh, wait till I get my hands on him," he said.

Clytie sat up and clutched at his sleeve as he tried to escape.

"Rodge!"

"You go on. I'll take this bastard and catch the next train to Omaha. For Christ's sake, let go!"

Clytie stood up, wide awake. "You never did mean to go to Omaha with me. What are you up to?"

"That man, he's a fugitive—"

"You lie. You ain't going to make a fool of me. You just took me along to keep me away from Charley Noble."

That did it. That gave him the nerve he needed to reach for the signal cord, just as the train started to move. Clytie still held his sleeve.

"Clytie, goddamnit, let go of me."

She let go. "All right, go on. You'll never see me again. This is the end."

The conductor opened the door at the end of the car as Downey raced down the aisle, unbuttoning his coat to get at his pearl-handled .45. "Fugitive. Go on with your train. I'll catch the next one," he said.

The conductor followed him as far as the steps. He leaned out to wave his signal to the engineer. Downey pulled the gun on the empty platform and charged about wildly, shouting, "Where'd he go, where's that fella, what became of that man?" The train moved, picked up speed, went out of sight.

CHAPTER 7

"But why come to me?" said Jerome Follansbee, president of the Merchants and Drovers Bank of Curtin.

"Because when I want to see how old a horse is, I don't go to his hind end. I look at his teeth," Sheriff Downey said boldly.

"I'd bet a pickle that you have all the information that we have, if not more. If you want to know whether the reward will really be paid—"

"I never had no idee it wouldn't."

"I reckon, then, that you have some reason to feel you'll collect it."

Downey merely nodded, as though this were not very important. He said nothing. There was a time to bet, and a time to check. And this dried-up, shriveled old geezer of a banker was too self-important to play a waiting game. He was guaranteed to fill any silences a man left.

He did. "I might say that the reward is being augmented, as soon as the paperwork is done."

"Augmented?" It was an unfamiliar word to Downey.

"Increased by fifteen hundred. Lord Dunconan is personally offering that much. I have his authorization, and the bank's lawyer is now drafting the public tender. You've heard of Lord Dunconan, of course."

"I heard there was some kind of English lord."

"Yes. Of the Fifty-one ranch."

"The Fifty-one? Only ranch I know with that mark is in Richardson County, Nebraska."

The banker smiled benignly. "Yes, Lord Dunconan owns

that one, too, but he is selling it and moving all his stock here."

"How come he's offering a reward?"

The banker hesitated, but he was dying to talk about his lordly friend, and Downey knew he had only to wait. "It is rather a family matter, but as an officer of the law, I'm sure you will use discretion," Follansbee said, proving Downey right. "Nylander offered Lord Dunconan's daughter an—an indignity. He insulted her."

"Fifteen hundred dollars' worth?"

"I should think so, Mr. Downey. He—he kept her out overnight. By force, you understand—by force! He—he took her riding and would not permit her to go home. Lady Phyllis, or to be more exact, the Honorable Phyllis Schoolfield, is a headstrong girl. She—she had been warned, but you know girls."

Downey was a little confused by all these names. "You mean," he said, "he kept her by force, but it didn't take very much."

Follansbee remained silent, but it was a silence of gentlemanly assent. Downey went on: "What I don't see is how this son of a bitch got to where he knowed a lord's daughter that well. How'd he get away with it?"

"Oh, he was working quite openly on the Fifty-one, as a horsebreaker, using the name of Tom Patterson. Very good man in his way, too. He broke a horse that Lord Dunconan sold to me. Splendid animal, handsomest I've ever driven, perfectly broke, and—"

"Just a minute. You mean that you know Chesty Bob Nylander, too?"

"Well, that is confidential, but it's true. I—"

"How did you find out it was Chesty Bob? How sure are you?"

"Oh, I'm sure enough! Two men who used to ride with Chesty Bob identified themselves to me. We needn't go into that, except that I paid them for their help. This was after Lady Phyllis, or I should say the Honorable Phyllis, had been kept out overnight—by force, you understand, by force! This 'Tom Patterson' had vanished, and somehow these two chaps heard about it and came to me. They described him perfectly. In fact, he had boasted to them that he was going to marry Lord Dunconan's daughter. You know, there is really no honor among thieves, is there? They wanted Chesty Bob killed."

"I reckon the lord did, too." Something hit Downey then. "Say! If you've seen Chesty Bob, you'd know him again if you saw him, wouldn't you?"

"Oh my, yes!"

"That's all I need, Mr. Follansbee, to gather him in. I know where he is and what he's doing and what name he's using, right now."

"No! Are you sure?"

"No question about it. I've got to go on to Omaha from here. When I get back I'm going to ask you to come to Hillary and identify this son of a bitch for me. I'll hit him like a ton of bricks, before he can make his move. Will you do that?"

Follansbee was trembling with eagerness. "All you have to do is telegraph me, and I'll catch the next train west. Certainly I owe that much to my old friend Lord Dunconan. It's my duty, too, of course. Where is he? He's a man of many disguises, you know. Posing as Tom Patterson, he wore a wig. Lady Phyllis, or, as I should say, the Honorable Phyllis, saw him take it off."

"That's the man, but I can't talk about it anymore right now. What I want to tell you is that I've been asked to run for lieutenant governor, and I'm just about in the notion to go for it."

"My word! What does Randy Crocker say?"

Downey grinned. "He don't hardly know what to say. I didn't ask him, I told him. If I arrest Chesty Bob Nylander, there's nobody Crocker can find that can beat me."

They talked a few minutes more. The old banker wanted

more facts about Chesty Bob, but he was not hard to put off, and Downey felt sure that what he had so far would not go past Lord Dunconan. Follansbee shook his hand at parting with far more cordiality than he had on arrival.

Downey stopped at the courthouse to pay his respects to Sheriff Andrew MacGowan, a young man serving his first term. MacGowan's deference elevated Downey's spirits, which were already high enough after his interview with the banker. I been too long humble, he told himself, plodding down toward the depot. Time I lived up to what I really am, a big man in this state. . . .

"I had to get off the Flyer suddenly this morning, and I left my stubs on the seat, with my wife," he told the passenger agent. "Have to ask you to make out a new ticket on the first train that'll get me to Omaha."

"Oh, I couldn't do that, stranger. You have no proof of purchase?"

"I was on a company ticket."

"You mean a pass?"

"You can't ride the palace car on a pass, and I was on the palace car, me and my wife. Wire your division headquarters. Ask the chief of detectives if I ain't entitled to replace the ticket that Louis Varden bought for me out of company funds. How long will that take?"

It took three hours, but he was an honored guest on a local train that would still get him to Omaha hours ahead of the next Flyer. It meandered purposefully across Nebraska, Downey staring out dully at the Platte Valley. He had not seen it for years, and he had hoped never to see it again. He had been a lot younger then, and had not known just how tough he really was.

Never again, never again . . . Most men, when they got to Downey's age, thought and talked about the men they had whipped and the women they had loved when they were twenty-two. The women Downey remembered had laughed at him, and the men had whipped him. All because he had not known how tough he could be, when he had to.

He changed trains twice, and the trains changed engines and crews several times. He arrived in Omaha early in the afternoon, descending the steps with a mob of tired, travel-stained travelers from the West. A slim young man with a mop of curly brown hair plucked at Downey's sleeve as he pushed through the crowd.

"I say there, Marshal Goodwin, remember me?" he said. "My, you look well! How's everything in Reno?"

The young man got in front of Downey, smiling into his face and clutching him by the lapels. "I ain't Marshal Goodwin and I ain't from Reno and I don't know you," Downey growled.

"My mistake. I apologize. I saw the twinkle of a badge under your coat, and it's years since I saw Marshal Goodwin, a man I admire as I did my own father. So sorry, so sorry!"

The personable young man vanished. It was not until an hour later that Downey discovered that his wallet had vanished, too. He was embarrassed at being picked for a country cop and angry at himself for falling for it, but being broke was a still more serious thing. He had only a dollar and eighty-two cents in silver in his pocket, and no idea where to find Clytie's family.

Omaha had grown enormously since he had last seen it. It awed him at first, and then cowed him. He walked its streets idly, like a vagabond cowboy—exactly as he had so many, many years ago, when he and this city were both a lot younger.

What he needed first was a drink. He turned back toward the river, and the cheaper saloons he knew would be found there. He peered into two or three, but all his self-confidence had ebbed away. A big man yesterday, he told himself, but just a bum today . . .

A familiar figure appeared halfway down the block, in a row of rundown frame buildings. It was a worthless cowboy whom Downey had caught in a strong-arm robbery in Hillary. The fellow was not big or strong, but he had speed and sheer viciousness. He had gone with one hand for the throat of another cowboy, and for the crotch with the other. Downey had not bothered to run him in. He remembered working him over so he'd know better than to come to Hillary again, and then putting him on his old eight-dollar horse and heading him out of town.

Another, smaller, ill-dressed man appeared. The two put their heads together for a moment, the one Downey knew doing all the talking. They walked swiftly down the street, perhaps thirty feet, and vanished into one of the wood-front buildings.

Downey backed around the corner. There had to be an alley in back of this block. He ran back and found it, and then walked swiftly down it, dodging trash and garbage. The first building with a back window was about where the two had gone in. He peered inside and saw stacked beer kegs and cases of bottled beer, and smelled the yeasty odor of a saloon.

The door was locked, but he braced one boot sole against the wall and jerked on the knob with both hands. The rotten wood yielded. He found himself in deep darkness the moment he slid around the first stack of kegs. He waited a moment, while his eyes accustomed themselves to the lack of light. He groped his way forward, found another doorknob, and turned it softly, slowly.

The door opened. He was looking into a saloon from the rear—empty, except for the fat bartender and the two youths he had seen on the sidewalk. The one Downey knew from Hillary was menacing the bartender with his own bungstarter.

"Come on, you pus-gut son of a bitch, let's have it."

"Boys, that's all there is. You got it all."

"Shit! Dey's a cotton bag full o' money, and I know it."

"I don't do that much business here. Boys, you don't want to go to the pen, do you? I'm willing to—"

"You're willin' to get your head broke open, dat's what."

The whelp raised the bungstarter. Downey wished he had his other gun, but the pearl-handled one would do. He thumbed back the hammer with a smile. It was not going to be the easiest shot in the world, but he knew exactly what would happen when he squeezed the trigger.

He squeezed. The gun jumped in his hand. The building echoed with its roar and Downey smelled the terrible, wonderful smell of burnt gunpowder. The whelp was left with a piece of splintered ash in his hand, as the hammer of the bungstarter exploded into shreds.

One of the youths screamed. Both sprinted for the door. Downey dropped another slug into the floor between and a little ahead of them, where they could see it. "Halt in your goddamn tracks!" he shouted.

They slid to a stop. He let them hear him cock the gun again as he shuffled toward them, grinning. He did not look at the bartender, but out of the corner of his mouth he grated, "Don't get between me and them, but go see if you can find a policeman."

"Yes, sir, and thanks a lot, sir. But watch that feller with the cowboy hat. He's pizen!"

"Him? Oh hell, me and him know each other real good," said Downey. "Don't we, you bastardly little son of a cockroach and a tarant'ler?"

The bartender flitted, all three hundred pounds of him, out the door. Downey made no threats to the two captives. He merely watched them.

Moments passed. "Say, I know you!" said the one who had wielded the bungstarter. Downey ignored him. He heard the shrill pealing of a police whistle coming closer and closer. The two captives measured their chances and did not like them.

A few minutes later the place was full of helmeted policemen. One of them was a burly sergeant, white-haired, but a big, powerful man, and more active than many a man of forty.

"Good shooting," he said, "but you know better than to come armed into Omaha. You'll have to come down to the station and explain that to somebody."

"Sure, Lloyd, I don't mind." Downey unbuttoned his coat to expose his sheriff's badge.

The sergeant squinted at it, and then at Downey. "Do I know you?"

"We worked together on a grading gang in Fort Scott, in— let's see, nineteen years ago this last summer."

"I don't place you, but I was there. You're sure-enough sheriff?"

"Sure enough."

"Well then, no way I can take you in, is they? Exchange of courtesies."

"I don't mind. I'd like to swab out my gun. Reckon I can do that there, can't I?"

"Anything we can do, the captain will do. This one son of a bitch is a bad one. He's got a record a mile long."

"Oh hell, he ain't bad," Downey said. "It's just the way his mama combs his hair that makes him look bad."

Downey was an honored guest at the station. While he swabbed his gun, drank coffee, and ate sandwiches and pie, messages went out at every opportunity to men on the beats. In less than an hour he had Barrington Tate's address. The captain offered to send Downey out in a departmental rig, but there was something Downey wanted to do first.

He returned to the saloon where he had captured the two stick-up men. Word had gotten around, and it was doing a good business, with two men on duty at the bar. Downey caught the eye of the one he had rescued and called him aside with a nod.

The bartender came, not willingly. "Didn't get a chance to thank you yet, sir, but I hope you'll let me give you a little gift," he said. He reached for his wallet even less willingly.

"Put away your money," Downey said. "There is one other thing you can do for me."

"Yes?" The fat bartender put his money away, but not his suspicions. "Anything I can do, sir."

"I need some of them there knockout drops."

"Them what, sir?"

"Quit stalling! The stuff you put in a man's liquor to put him to sleep, and don't tell me you haven't got any because I goddamn well know better."

"Oh, chloral hydrate. What in the world do you want with that stuff, sir? It's dangerous!"

"So is a Colt forty-five, but I had one when you needed me to have one, didn't I?"

The fat man sighed. "Listen, that goddamn Henry Goodenow didn't send you down here to buy this stuff, did he?"

"Who?"

"That sergeant, Henry Goodenow. Hey, listen—you wouldn't deadfall me like that, would you?"

"You must be close to feeble-minded, to think you can talk to a Wyoming sheriff like that."

"Excuse it. I'll be right back, sir."

The bartender was back in a minute, with a small brown bottle. "I don't like to give you the full-strength, but I ain't got another bottle. You be careful with this stuff! Three drops will put a man out for several hours. You can kill somebody easy with too much."

The label on the bottle was fresh, and the cork was sealed with red wax. Downey put it in his pocket, with his handkerchief, and returned to the station. There, the burly, white-haired sergeant was waiting to drive him to Barrington Tate's place.

It was a pleasant drive southward, on a winding paved road that overlooked the river most of the way. The Tate place was a big, sprawling farmhouse that badly needed painting and a general clean-up. Several rigs stood in a row in front of it, the horses that had pulled them resting, unharnessed, in a lot behind the house. A multitude of children were playing in the yard, with the subdued gaiety to be expected with death in the house.

Downey thanked the sergeant and got out of the departmental buggy.

"You know," the sergeant said, "I been trying to place a Rodge Downey from Fort Scott. Only whack I can make at remembering the name is a skinny little piss-ant that was scared of his shadow."

"You remember, all right," Downey said. "You may be Henry Goodenow now, but you was Lloyd Diehl then. What I remember is you beating that poor son of a bitch of a Canadian up with a shovel. You was a dirty, cowardly bully then and I reckon you still are, and if you make one move toward that gun, I'll shove it up your ass and kick the handle off."

He turned his back on the sergeant, opened the gate, and swaggered up to the front door. He heard the sergeant turn the buggy and chirp the horse into a trot, and he knew he had just won an unexpected, and therefore sweeter, victory over the past.

CHAPTER 8

The trip home was endless, and as tiresome as the week spent in Omaha. He could not wait to get back and close to the problem that was also his opportunity. He knew exactly what he was going to do, and was tense with his eagerness to get at it.

Clytie, sulking beside him in the palace car, was another problem, one to be settled at leisure. There had been a long, low-voiced but passionate discussion when they met at Uncle Barrington's house. Grandma had died the evening before. Her body lay in the dark parlor. Downey counted fifty-four Tates, sleeping in and about the house. He had not expected to be welcomed.

But he was. Clytie had not been able to resist announcing that he was to run for lieutenant governor, and the Tates were almost servile in their respect. He could not get Clytie alone until after the funeral, in which he was made conspicuously one of the chief mourners, and then they had to talk in the woodshed with a late, hard rain battering the tin roof. Clytie hugged herself and shivered, declining to meet his eyes.

"You shamed me in front of the train crew. You never did have no intention of coming with me! I'm through."

"I had to do my duty," he said virtuously. "And listen, Clytie, the hell of it is, I can't say it'll never happen again. That's the life of a law officer."

"Where's the fugitive you went after, then?"

"He got away. If you hadn't hung on to me—"

"I don't believe you. I'm going to tell Uncle Barrington that we're separating."

But she lacked the nerve to do that. They slept that night on a pallet in the kitchen, Clytie with her back to him. Downey arose in the dark to build up the fire in the big range and make coffee in the strange pot. Old, stringy, creaking Uncle Barrington came in for a cup, in his long underwear. He pinned Downey down for an hour and a half, to recount every ache and pain in his lean body. To Downey, he looked exceedingly fit and well rested.

Breakfast was an orderly madhouse. The children were fed first, on floors in every room—pancakes, fried side-meat, fried eggs in heaps. By the time the first adults sat down, with Downey at the head of the table, he had this enormous clan figured out.

"Excuse me, but ain't there going to be no grace said before meat? There's been a good old woman took from us, and a word of prayer is in order, ain't it?" he said.

"You'd've heard prayer if you'd got here in time," Clytie said. Her uncle reproached her with a spaniellike glance, and then led them in a meandering baritone prayer that Grandma not forget them in Heaven. From that moment, Clytie was stifled. She dared not say a word against her own husband.

The food the Tates packed for their return trip was only half gone when the train pierced the hills around Hillary. He busied himself getting their things together. Clytie watched him until he was sure everything was at hand and could sit down again.

"Well, Rodge, I didn't have a good time, but I guess a person ain't expected to at a time like that. I'm just plain homesick," she said.

"So am I."

"Everything will be a mess, but I ain't going to pitch in until tomorrow."

"Work is always there when you get to it, Clytie."

"I guess you're pretty mad at me, ain't you?"

"No. You plague the hell out of me sometimes, but I don't blame you. A sheriff is married to his job, I reckon."

The train was slowing down for the station, and she did not have to answer. Familiar faces were waiting for them on the depot platform. The last one sported a big red steerhorn mustache and an expensive auburn-brown wig. Charley Noble was still here, and peace came to Downey's soul. That was the one thing he had feared—that Chesty Bob Nylander's plans would have matured to a new phase that moved him out of town.

"How did everybody know we was coming on this train?" he asked, descending the steps.

"Why, I believe the UP detective arranged it so the agent would be telegraphed when you boarded the train. Folks is plumb proud to have you back, Mr. Downey—and you too, Mrs. Downey. I hope it wasn't the sad occasion you feared when you left."

Clytie's big lower lip trembled as she met that wig-wearing, bank-robbing bastard's eyes. "Grandma was sinking fast when I got there. She didn't know me, but I was holding her hand when she died."

"It's something that comes to all of us," Downey said. He tried to elbow Charley aside, but the master of disguise would not step out of the limelight. He had both of their suitcases in charge by the time Downey had shaken all the hands. Downey had to wrestle him for them.

"You didn't have to be so mean," Clytie said as he followed her up the hill, carrying both valises.

"He's got his own business to run. I don't need nobody's help."

"Get him mad, and then where is that three dollars a week coming from?"

"Woman, don't you ever think of anything but money?"

She did not answer. He opened the door and went in ahead of her. He put the valises down in the musty-smelling living room, and he and his wife gazed at each other without kindness. Downey was the first to turn his eyes. Trapped, he was thinking. Trapped, by God, after the way I've worked all my life to lift myself up by my bootstraps. I count for something in this state, but does it mean anything to her? The hell it does . . .

He raised blinds that Charley had lowered, stirred up fires that Charley had banked, opened windows to let out the stale air that Charley had already breathed. He took off his dress gun and holster and changed to his workaday coat. When he came out of their bedroom, Clytie was standing in the kitchen, staring dully at the clock in her hand. It was not running.

Downey had set his watch with the conductor's that morning. He took the clock, wound it, and set it: 4:34 P.M. Clytie seemed to be in a sullen daze. She stared at the shoe boxes full of uneaten sandwiches and fried chicken left over from their return trip.

"What'll I do with all this food, Rodge?"

"Feed it to the chickens—if you've got any chickens left."

"I sure wouldn't want no more of it. Will you be hungry for supper when you come home?"

He almost exploded. "How the hell do I know how hungry I'm going to be?"

He stalked out of the house. Constable Miller Mahaffey was lurking in the front yard, leaning against a tree to rest, as he always said, his wooden leg. He pegged along beside Downey, reporting all that had happened in the past week. Mamie Scheidert had had the washing stolen from her clothesline and a haystack burned. Doc Lavoey was dickering for the lot next to Pengill's, and was thinking of building his own building and taking in a partner. Hugh Dean was going around calling Downey "Governor," and when people asked him what he meant, he only laughed and said, "Rodge is going to run for lieutenant governor. They'll have to change the locks on the governor's office to keep old Rodge out, if he makes it."

"Rodge," Miller panted, "is that right, are you going to run?"

"Oh, there's talk of it, but I ain't made up my mind. I wish Hugh didn't talk so much."

"Did you talk to the governor in Cheyenne?"

"No, I didn't."

"Everybody figgers you did."

"I can't help what people think. Where the hell is Monte Barrett?"

"He rode out to talk to the Widow Scheidert."

He did not have to ask about the prisoner, Chet Wilson. They were at the courthouse door, and Wilson was lonesomely playing his harmonica in his cell. But Downey exploded with anger at the condition of the yard around the outside entrance to his office. The debris of the windstorm that had occurred on the day of his departure for Omaha had piled up against the wall, and there it still lay.

The harmonica music ceased. Downey went into his office, closing the door in Miller Mahaffey's face. It was a comfort to sort through the mail that had piled up in his absence, especially so when he found the circular that Jerome Follansbee had mentioned. Lord Dunconan was not mentioned in it. The $1,500 reward was being offered by the Merchants and Drovers Bank of Curtin, acting as trustee.

"Hey, Mist' Downey, you back?" came the voice of the prisoner.

Downey slid the mail into the top drawer of his desk. "Sure I am, and you're going to catch hell from now on," he said. He got up and went back into the cellblock, somehow remembering poignantly how it felt to be friendless, helpless, and confined. The prisoner's shorn head made him look truly pitiful. A poor man got used to indignities, but deep in his heart they still stung.

"I guess you must be about the meanest old sheriff in the world," Wilson said.

Downey chuckled. "Prob'ly. Just mean enough to get you out of that cell and put you to work tomorrow morning, cleaning up the weeds and leaves and limbs that blowed in. If anybody throwed a match into it, this whole courthouse would burn up, with you in it."

The prisoner pulled up the leg of his pants. "I can't do no work with this wound. Look, sir."

Downey looked. "'Pears fine to me. A little work will do it good. Had your supper yet?"

"No, and I didn't have breakfast until noon. That Monte is just plain worthless, you know that?"

"You're a great one to talk about worthless."

Downey made up his mind suddenly to eat at Tong Ti's. It would keep him away from Clytie, and postpone for a while the inevitable showdown, and it would give him a chance to regain touch with his people and his town. He promised to send a meal to Wilson from the restaurant and went out, locking the office door behind him.

Just as he turned from locking it and walked down the short corridor to the outer door, it opened and Lena Barrett came in. She paused, with the door open behind her. It did not illuminate her face, but it outlined her sumptuous body and threw a halo over her pale hair.

"Gee, Mr. Downey, you back?" she said, letting the door close. It was almost pitch-dark in the corridor. If she didn't know he was coming in today, she was the only person in Hillary who didn't. . . .

"Yes. What can I do for you, Lena?" he said. His voice came out—at least to his own ears—unsteady, breathy, ready to break into a squeak. He could see her face, now that his eyes were used to the dim light. He could actually smell her, the sweet and musky essence of girl that a man's nose never got too old to pick up. Especially, he thought, in the dark . . .

"I wonder when Monte will be back, and whether I ought to fix supper at the regular time."

"Depends on what your regular time is. You—you want to wait here in the office for him?"

"No, he don't like me to hang around here," Lena said, and he took note that her own voice was unsteady.

"Why not? Afraid I'll steal you, or what?"

"Oh gee whiz, Mr. Downey! He just don't think it's my place."

"You know, Lena, I'd steal you if I could," he said. "But I bet you knowed that all along, didn't you?"

He took a step toward her. She retreated to the door. She clasped her white, white hands together between her big breasts—and how white they must be, too! Her eyes half closed. The tip of her tongue came out far enough to dampen her lips.

"I—I better get home. What time is it?" she said.

He put his hands on her shoulders. "Plenty of time, if you know what I mean. I—I'll leave a note for Monte to stay here until I get back. Oh lordie, Lena, you're so pretty, and the way you look at a man—"

"Oh Jesus, Mr. Downey, you don't know what you're saying! Oh God, let me go, please let me go!" she whimpered.

He dropped his hands. He shook himself like a dog coming out of the water, shaking off the illusions that could have made him seven kinds of a jackass. Still could, if she ever talked. The worst thing he could do, instinct said, was act scared or ashamed.

"Well sure, Lena, but if you don't want a man to ask you, don't roll your eyes at him, and don't shake your butt like you do. You don't do yourself or Monte any credit, either one, the flirty way you act in Tong Ti's," he said.

"Oh God, do I? I do not!"

"I just wonder why Monte puts up with it. There's two kinds of women, Lena. You *say* you're one kind, but you *act* like the other. By God, it is just that simple!"

He opened the door for her and let her escape. He felt like crossing himself, the way he had seen Catholics do after a narrow escape from danger. A man with a wife as cantankerous as Clytie had to get it out of his system some way. But Lena Barrett sure wasn't the way.

He gave Lena time to go a block or two, and came out just in time to face Louie Varden. The detective was not alone. The stranger with him was a burly man with the shoulders and arms of an ape, and the battered ears and eyebrows of an old prizefighter. Louie Varden was the last man in the world Downey wanted to meet now, but he fetched a smile and offered his hand.

"Rodge, meet Tom Fink, the Camden Bulldog—or, as I should say, the Reverend Tom Fink," Varden said. "Tom, shake hands with Rodgerson Downey, our most famous sheriff, and, for all we know, our next lieutenant governor."

"Why, I've long been an admirer of the manly art," Downey said, "and everybody knows the Camden Bulldog."

The old fighter folded both of his big, bruised hands around Downey's, saying, in a hoarse voice, "Brother, I have put all that behind me. I have felt the countenance of the forgiving God to shine upon me, and I want to share the blessings with the fine people of—what town is this?"

"Hillary. It's some time since there's been a revival here, but you better talk to the preachers first. I don't take that in my jurisdiction."

"Yes, Lord, I'll do that. But first I must strengthen the spirit of a man who has called to me out of the pit of hell. Which way, Mr. Detective?"

The three moved off together under Varden's direction. "It's that fiddler, Feathers, Rodge," the detective said. "He has been liquoring up ever since you left here. Tom has got him about dried out, but when I seen Fiddler, he looked ready to dip his beak again."

The fiddler was sitting on Erik Sontag's steps, impeding customers, in violation of the statutes, but Downey did not interfere. The former Camden Bulldog sat down beside the wretched musician, put his arms around him, and soon had him on his feet. Over the fiddler's head, he smiled reassuringly at Downey and Varden. The two moved on.

"What I wonder," Downey said, "is what the hell has kept you here all this time, Louie."

"Oh, I been in and out, in and out. We're setting up that code system Hugh Dean suggested. Rodge, have you et yet?"

"No, I'm just heading for the Chinyman's."

"I wonder if your good woman couldn't fix us a bait, so we could talk in private."

With Chesty Bob in the next room, maybe? I guess not. . . . "No, she's tired from her trip. But I can ask Tong Ti to let us eat in the back room. Ain't everybody he'd do it for, but he will for me."

The restaurant was busy, but at a wink from Downey the proprietor unlocked a door behind the counter. They passed through into a neat little dining room, with doilies cut from white paper under the plates, and paper flowers in vases on the tables. Tong Ti lighted two lamps.

"Now, this is on me, Rodge," Varden warned. "I don't want to see you reaching for your money."

Downey first ordered a meal sent down to the jail for his prisoner, bringing a small grimace of agony from Varden. The detective ordered chicken and dumplings, but after two long trips on the train, Downey had had all the chicken he wanted for a while. He asked for a porterhouse steak, fried potatoes, a sliced onion, and, in afterthought, two fried eggs.

Varden fell on his food like a wolf for a few moments. It seemed to Downey that he was eating the way a man smoked when he was nervous—hard and fast, in search of strength and steady nerves. Varden looked up at last, his mouth full of food and his eyes full of pain.

"Rodge," he said, "why don't you come clean with me? What are you keeping from me?"

"The question," Downey said in a hard voice, "is what you're keeping from me. You come in here hoping to split a reward that *I'll* have to earn, while *you* set on your hind end back in Cheyenne in your office. And you only tell me what I already know, not one goddamn word more."

"Rodge, I swear that I—"

"Oh, the hell with that! How about Lord Dunconan and his reward? Hey, that catched you right in the belly, didn't it? You thought you'd hog that yourself, didn't you?"

Varden held up his right hand. "Rodge, I swear I didn't know His Lordship was offering a reward."

"You didn't even know about Honorable Phyllis getting spread out in the hay by Chesty Bob, did you?"

"Oh Jesus, nobody's supposed to know that!"

"Well, I know it, and I know a hell of a lot more. And when the time is right, Chesty Bob Nylander is going to think the Fourth Cavalry has fell on him in ranks of four, at the gallop. And if I split the reward with anybody, it'll be with my own fellow citizens who help me take him, not with somebody sitting at a desk and practicing to be a snake in the grass."

"Rodge, surely my information is worth something to you!"

"You didn't give me no information that I didn't already have."

Varden slammed his fork down on his plate. He had gone white of face, and his hard slash of a mouth dribbled spit at both corners. He choked, "There's no fool like an old fool, they say. I don't know how I expected good sense from an old man that can't even run his own house. If I had a young wife, and a horny young boarder like—"

Whap!

It sounded like a pistol shot in the closed room as Downey raised himself just high enough to catch Varden across his left cheek with a heavy, open hand. Varden's chair went over backward. Downey almost upset the table in his haste to get around it. A half-stunned Varden was fumbling in his armpit for his gun. Downey put his big foot on the detective's wrist.

"Don't do it, Louie! Don't force me to shoot you in my own town, with my own witnesses."

Varden lay on his side on the floor, until he had his wits back.

"I made a bad mistake, Rodge. Let me up."

Downey let him stand up and dust off his clothing. "You won't believe this," Varden said in a trembling voice, "but I ain't thinking half as much about the reward as I am about Chesty Bob outsmarting all of us and robbing the UP."

"You're right, I don't believe it."

Varden closed his eyes hopelessly. "I'm out of a job forever if it happens."

"It ain't going to happen," Downey said. "Put it out of your mind. You may not believe this, either, but I'm going to have Chesty Bob in chains, right in my own jail, and sooner than you think."

"You're right about that," Varden said. "I don't believe it."

CHAPTER 9

Downey slept badly that night, in his own bed, with Clytie sleeping heavily beside him with her face to the wall. There was a bright sky and a heavy frost when he got up at sunrise. While he was shaving, Clytie got up and began cooking his breakfast. He was too nervous to be hungry—too aware of the little brown bottle in his hip pocket, with his handkerchief. What it represented was the most important thing he had to do, but it was not the only one.

There was a westbound freight that was due into Hillary at 4:14, but it was just whistling into town as Downey finished breakfast. No word had been spoken so far. None was spoken now as he reached for his hat and coat, although he could hear Charley Noble stretching and yawning and making his bed creak in the lean-to off the kitchen. He tried to meet Clytie's eyes several times before leaving the house. She was always looking somewhere else.

The ice was an inch thick on the town horse trough near the Hillary State Bank. Ben Chase, its president, was just coming down the street, wearing the old buffalo coat his father had worn for so many years.

"Skipping out with the boodle before the town is awake, Ben?" Downey asked him, as he smashed the ice in the trough with a handy rock and began pumping fresh water into the trough.

Chase, with a .45 in his desk drawer and the heavy second-generation tradition bending his legs, did not like humor. "Judge Dilham's wife died, didn't you hear?" he said.

"No, I didn't. How did that get you out of bed?"

"Jim Lavoey came over to ask Nettie to sit up with her about midnight. Jim had to go on another case. It was hopeless, but you can't leave a man alone at a time like that."

Ben went into his bank. Downey went straight to the judge's house. Dr. Lavoey's old bay mare dozed under a blanket, tied to a tree in the front yard. When Downey knocked, Nettie Chase came to the door. She had been a nurse in an Omaha hospital when Ben had met her. She was not one of Downey's friends, but she was one of the people he respected in this town.

"The judge is asleep. He's exhausted, and the doctor finally got him to lie down," she said.

"I wouldn't bother him. I just wonder if I could see the doctor a minute."

"I'll see." The woman closed the door in his face and vanished. In a moment she returned. "He'll be here in a moment. Please come in, Sheriff."

Her soft-voiced formality cowed him. She was not a pretty woman, but she had a presence, a decency, that made him yearn for her approval. "No, thanks, Nettie. Only take a minute. I'll wait here."

"As you wish."

She closed the door. It was several minutes before Dr. Lavoey opened it. "Yes, Rodge?"

"When do you figger the funeral will be, Doc?"

"Day after tomorrow, probably. I'm embalming the remains now. Why?"

"The judge has a pair of graves in the graveyard. Nobody ever thinks of digging the grave until the last minute. The ground is freezing fast. Seems to me it'd be a good idee to get the grave dug. Take that off'n his hands."

"Why, Rodge, that's very thoughtful. I'll get the number of the plot he wants opened, and see that you get it, will you? You'll be able to find a couple of men to do it for a dollar or two each, and Roy will see that you get it back. He'll be so appreciative."

"Don't even mention it to him, and don't worry about the money. There's always these dirty damn jobs that nobody ever thinks of when there's a death, it always seems, and I usually wind up doing them."

"I guess you do, at that. There's a lot of things you do that we'd miss if you stopped doing them. I'll let you know about the grave, Rodge."

It was warming up rapidly as the sun's rays reached the street. Downey saw Louie Varden pacing up and down on the cinder platform of the depot to keep warm as he waited for the freight train to finish its switching. Downey waved and shouted at him.

"Hey, Louie!"

The detective merely waved back, and then changed his mind. Leaving his bag on the platform, he hurried to meet Downey near the courthouse.

"Are we still friends?" he asked.

"Why, I sure hope so," said Downey. "I don't know why we shouldn't be."

"Well, I opened my big mouth last night and—"

"If anything like that happened, I've already forgot what it was. The main thing you and me has got to do, Louie, is just capture the worst outlaw since Jesse James, that's all."

"Well, there's that reward, you know."

"You help me, you'll share in it. I'll see to it."

"But I have helped you."

"Not yet you haven't. One thing you can do, you can put me on the list to get that code number on the money train."

"I'll try, but it's asking too much." Varden looked down and drew a circle in the cold dust with the toe of his boot. "I have to do what I'm told, Rodge."

"Then you foller your conscience and I'll foller mine when it comes time to split the rewards."

The train hooted an answer to an unseen conductor's signal —*highball*. Varden had to sprint to catch up his bag and catch the caboose on the fly. His only answer was a half-hearted wave of the hand.

Monte Barrett and Miller Mahaffey were ambling toward the courthouse. The sheriff waited for them at the door. He pointed at the storm debris piled against the courthouse wall.

"Look at that mess, Monte."

"I know. What we need is a team to haul it off," said Monte.

Downey said wrathfully, "It ain't our job to haul it off. Just get it to hell away from the wall, so it don't burn us down if somebody throws a cigar butt into it. Get that prisoner out with a pitchfork and make him pile it over yonder. He don't eat breakfast until it's done."

"I don't know if he should be doing work like that, with his bad leg."

"The hell with his leg. It'll be good for it. Miller, you take a shotgun out of the rack and help Monte bluff that boy into turning out a day's work. I'll tell Tong Ti to send some breakfast down when he hears from you that the job is done."

He unlocked the office and led the way inside. He let Monte handle the prisoner, until he heard Wilson's squalls of protest about his bad leg. Downey jumped up and shouted back into the cellblock:

"Get up off your rump, boy, and look lively, you hear? Monte, put about three feet of chain on his good ankle, that's all. If he can't work a pitchfork with that, make it six. Here, Miller, I'll get you a gun. One barrel buck, and one birdshot. And don't fool around with him! I want to see that shave-headed boy work."

"I can see it ain't going to be no winter resort in this jail," the prisoner said cheerfully. "All right, who am I to make a fuss? Just nobody, just nobody."

Downey chuckled gruffly. "The way you eat, you ain't no nobody. I'll send you up some more pancakes when the job is done."

"Oh boy, pancakes!"

Downey handed Miller a double-barreled shotgun and four shells, two loaded with buckshot, two with birdshot. He locked the gun rack and stamped out of the office without waiting to see them bring the prisoner out, but he could hear the dull jangle of the short chain that Monte had locked on the poor, witless cowboy's leg.

Charley Noble was just opening the De Luxe, puffing on a thick, black cigar. He hailed Downey with an upraised hand and a deferential, toothy smile.

"Hidy, Mr. Downey."

"Morning, Charley."

"Making your morning rounds, I see. Everybody feels safer, knowing Sheriff Downey is on the job."

Downey grunted and hurried on. In front of the Hillary Hotel, a noble horse with a 51 brand was tied. It had been sleekly curried and brushed, and was restless from inactivity. It would be a real pleasure, Downey thought wistfully, to ride the ginger out of that horse on a bright, cold morning like this. But it ain't for me. . . .

The Camden Bulldog came down the steps, one arm around Fiddler Feathers. The fiddler had his fiddle in one hand, his bedroll in the other. He looked woebegone, but otherwise not in bad shape for a man who had been drinking hard for over a week.

"Leaving us, Mr. Feathers?" Downey asked.

Fiddler smiled wanly and gulped a couple of times. "Brother Feathers," said the evangelical ex-pug, "is persuaded that there is only temptation for him here. He is riding on, Sheriff Downey."

"He'll find the same temptation everywhere."

"But he leaves old associations behind, and he takes with him the spirit of the Lord like an angel hovering over him."

Downey smiled skeptically. "Reckon he'll need it. I ain't sorry to see you go, Fiddler, but on the average, you'll find less temptation here than any other town I know."

"I realize that, Mr. Downey," the musician said in a trembling voice, "but I'm too ashamed to stay here. I make my living fiddling for the public, and how can I ask people to support me when they have seen me drunk?"

"By being sober, that's how. Would you think about making a deal for that horse before you go?"

"I—I couldn't part with my horse, Sheriff. A man is less than he was, when he sells a good horse."

"Something in that, all right."

Downey gave the departing penitent a civil wave and walked on. Erik Sontag stopped to complain about cowboys and loafers sitting on the steps to his store and making it necessary for his customers to pick their way through.

"You need wider steps and a double door."

"What? You expect me to spend a lot of money to accommodate a lot of loafers?"

"No, I don't. I don't even expect you to spend any to accommodate your customers. I've seen powder-houses where it was easier to get in for a box of dynamite than it is for a woman to come in there and buy a month's bait of groceries. But you're a tightwad, and it don't mean nothing to you that a working man hasn't got a place to set down on the street. I try to keep this town so a good man looking for a job will want to come back when the ranchers need him, and a hell of a lot of help you are! Some of the cattlemen ought to know about this."

"You have always bought from me, and my wife buys our family milk and eggs from you. I don't understand this attitude."

Downey had not known that Clytie was selling eggs to the Sontags, too. "I can buy somewhere else and you can get your milk and eggs somewhere else, if I have to listen to you bellyaching to get along with you, Erik. By God, a man with all the money you've got—"

A shotgun boomed.

A man shouted.

Another man screamed.

Downey was a block and a half from the courthouse. He pulled his .45 and began running toward it, pushing Sontag violently out of the way.

A rider on a fine horse was riding recklessly toward the tracks. His close-clipped head was bare, and the length of chain swinging from his ankle only stirred that horse to more splendid effort. How he could run! Downey held his breath and came to a complete stop, as the fine 51 gelding set sail over the first side-track. He cleared it like a bird.

He took the main line in the same fashion, the hatless rider leaning low over the horse's withers and whooping in its shot-back ears. The gelding took the other two tracks like a steeplechaser, vanished down the creek bank at a dead run, and half appeared again as it leaped the frozen creek.

Then it was gone in the trees, beyond which there was one wire fence with a wooden gate. The rider would see the gate in time to lift the horse over it, Downey felt sure. He only wished he could see that beautiful jump. Beyond, there was open range.

How five men could create the impression of an immense, disorderly horde was simply too much to understand. Miller Mahaffey was stumping about on his wooden leg and babbling incoherently. Fiddler Feathers kept bawling, "My horse, my horse, he stole my horse!" The erstwhile Camden Bulldog was trying to calm Feathers by shouting exhortations in his ear, and was only making things worse. The big, bully-ing cowboy who had already caused Downey trouble, Joe Ogren, was pulling at Downey's sleeve and shouting in his ear, "I seen it all, I seen it all, I seen it all."

Monte Barrett, while not calm, at least could tell what had happened. He pointed an accusing finger at Fiddler Feathers, but he almost sobbed as he talked.

"It was that goddamn fool's fault, Mr. Downey. He thought Wilson had busted jail, and he tried to take Miller's shotgun away from him to kill that poor ignorant cowboy with a chain on his leg. The sot, the soak, the damn ignorant fool, all he done was scare that horse to death. Did you see him run? Oh my, how he can run!"

"Shut up," Downey said. "How about that, Fiddler? You trying to land your butt in jail, or what?"

"I seen that man outside. What do you expect a man to think when he sees a prisoner outside? You have let him steal a horse that cost me two hundred and ninety dollars. This is what comes of letting him out of jail."

Downey took an iron grip on Fiddler's arm and made him wince. "Fiddler, where's your fiddle?"

"Yonder." Feathers pointed to where he had dropped it on the brush that Chet Wilson had piled.

"All right, you pick it up and start walking out of town."

"I can't leave town. He stole my horse."

"Throw him in, Monte. Book him for interfering with an officer, putting an officer in peril, stealing an officer's firearm— all felonies. If I can think of any more, I'll write it down before he goes to court."

Tom Fink, the Camden Bulldog, appealed to him. "Sheriff, I beg you to give me a chance with this poor fellow. I'll have him on the next train out of town, when I go. I'll tend him as the Samaritan did the stricken wayfarer."

"I ain't leaving without my horse," Feathers said. "I'd ruther go to jail."

"I haven't got your horse. I'm going to send Monte out to try to track him down, as soon as he can find some help. He'll be here if we can find him. You ain't going to help none, laying here in jail."

"Come, brother," Fink urged.

Downey clapped the fiddler on the shoulder. "Do as the reverend says, boy. You don't know when you're well off. Go on, Mr. Fink—get him out of here."

The old prizefighter linked arms with Fiddler, with a fine specimen of the grip the sheriff knew as a "come along." A thumb applied to the fiddler's wrist brought a soft moan of pain, and he trotted along meekly. At a nod from Downey, Monte loped off to search for men anxious to take a pleasant ride for a dollar a day. Miller Mahaffey, fearing the worst, handed over the shotgun and the three shells that had not been fired.

"That's the way it goes, Miller," Downey said, laughing. "You can protect people against everything but their own foolishness. Come on, let's clean this gun up and forget it happened."

"You—you ain't mad, Rodge?"

"Me? Way I figure it, we got two problems off'n our hands, this prisoner and that drunken fiddler."

He sent the constable on his way, happy and grateful. He closed the office and put his mind to his most pressing problem by detouring past the De Luxe Barber Shop. A glance in the window showed him Charley Noble in his own chair, reading a tattered book.

It was exactly what he had hoped to find, without any expectation of finding it. He turned in, and Charley leaped to his feet with a toothy and conciliatory smile.

"Hidy, Mr. Downey. Shave?"

"Well, Charley, what I really came for, I wonder if you have a drink around here. I just had a prisoner escape, the funniest damn thing you ever seen. I can use a snort, but I don't want to go into no saloon and have to answer a lot of damn-fool questions."

Charley rolled his prominent eyes conspiratorially. "I'll show you where I hide a bottle of the best, Mr. Downey, and I'm going to give you a key so you can slip in here anytime you feel the need of a nip. You come here."

The sheriff's heart leaped. He followed Charley back into the bath house, and through it to the boiler room, where the tall, cast-iron monstrosity sighed away with its fire banked. Charley reached back behind a sway-brace that angled across the wall studs and brought out a quart bottle of bonded, ten-year-old whiskey. Not more than a drink or two had been taken from it.

"Say, Charley, that's slick!"

"You treat that as your own bottle, Mr. Downey."

The sheriff, to whom liquor had never been either problem or boon, drank sparingly. He handed the bottle back.

"That's good whiskey. Well, as the Irishman says, some whiskey is better than others, but it's all good."

"Yes, sir, that ain't no joke."

"Charley, you know when I most appreciate a little nip?"

"No, when is that?"

"On a cold morning, early, before breakfast."

"That's when I like a nip, myself. Sometimes, anyway."

"Tell you what, I'll bring a couple of glasses down from the house, one for you and one for me, and I'll take a drink with you when we can. A man hates to drink alone."

"That sure is the truth."

"The next bottle is mine."

"Oh, this one will last a long time! You just put the glasses there with the bottle. Here, I'll get you a key to the front door."

"Mighty obliging, Charley."

"Proud to do it, proud to do it."

Downey put the key on his ring and escaped. He went straight to the depot.

"What held up the early-morning freight today?" he asked the agent.

"There's a slow order on for forty miles, where they're rebuilding some track."

"This train going to be late every day now?"

"For a while. Not this late, though. About five-thirty is when we can usually expect it."

"What's the number of it?"

He took a telegraph blank and wrote a message to be sent

to Jerome Follansbee, president of the Merchants and Drovers Bank of Curtin, Wyoming. It said:

CAN YOU TAKE FREIGHT TRAIN NO 1848 DAY AFTER TOMORROW ON PROPOSITION I MENTIONED WILL MEET YOU AT TRAIN DON'T SAY A WORD TO NOBODY.

"And don't you say nothing to nobody, either, and the minute an answer comes, get it to me," he told the agent.

He was somehow glad to get out of the depot. Now that he had set in motion the showdown, his nerves were suddenly screaming. His entire future depended upon the outcome of this affair.

He saw Monte gallop out, followed by three town loafers. He found two more, and led them to Dr. Lavoey's office. He then personally escorted them to the cemetery, found the right gravesite, and set them to digging with picks, shovels, and crowbars to pierce the frozen topsoil.

He saw two Indian youths tying in front of Erik Sontag's store, and stopped to question them in friendly fashion. Both were working cowhands—both were Arapahos—both were scowlingly resentful.

"You boys aim to buy something here?"

"We might, and we might not," one said.

"This old skinflint charges everybody too much, but he's just hell on Indians. Want I should go in with you and kind of look over your shoulder?"

"What good would that do?"

"Well, he knows that my wife is half Arapaho, and he damn well knows how I feel about things. Come on!"

He saw the boys through their purchases from a merchant so nervous that he lopped forty cents off the bill and then gave each boy a bag of tobacco. Downey walked out with them, nodded genially, and started away.

"I heard about you," one boy said.

"So did I," said the other.

"Nothing too bad, I hope."

"They say you give an Indian a fair shake."

"Boys, I give everybody a fair shake. I'll throw your asses in jail as quick as anybody else. But I'm the sheriff for all the people, and don't you never forget it!"

Having a half-Arapaho wife would probably get him votes, even among the white men. The Araps had had their troubles in Colorado. A lot of them were killed, others lost everything in Cavalry burn-outs, still others left the tribal life and worked in the white man's world. There were Arapaho traders and teamsters and harness-makers, and not a few who owned their own cattle ranches.

Monte Barrett came to the house as Downey was eating supper that evening, after dark. "We follered his sign for quite a piece," he reported, "but he had the horse on us, and that's about the size of it. That gelding could fly! He's long gone in the hills, I'm afeared."

"Forget it, Monte. Day after tomorrow, now, I want you to turn up in your best clothes. We've got to go to Mrs. Dilham's funeral."

"You bet. I'll bring my wife, too. What time is it?"

"I don't know."

"You going to bring your wife?"

Downey did not look around at Clytie. "Yes."

When Monte had gone, Clytie confronted him. "I hate to go to funerals and I didn't know the judge's wife."

"All the more reason to pay your respects."

"I ain't going, Rodge."

"You're going. You may go with your hands roped together behind you, but, by God, this is one time I'm going to have my wife with me. And you'll hold on to my arm part of the time, and let me open doors for you and so forth. And wear something good, Clytie. You can be the best-looking woman there if you try."

"All right, I'll go." She studied him, shaking her head wonderingly. "I never will understand you, Rodge. A body could almost think you're proud of me sometimes."

"Yes," he said, "they could, couldn't they?"

CHAPTER 10

It was a relief to be rid of Chet Wilson and have a quiet office the next morning. Monte was out serving tax-delinquent notices, making himself a few extra dollars but spending most of it on a rented horse and buggy. He had Lena and the baby along with him for an outing. Downey worried only a little over what Lena might say to his deputy. He had larger matters on his mind.

Tomorrow was the day. He parted his coat to pluck his watch from his vest pocket. Nine-fifty, and by this time to-morrow he'd have the goods on Chesty Bob and the handcuffs and leg-chains besides.

Little light came into the office through the windows, and he had not lighted the lamps. The dump needed cleaning; have to mount Monte with spurs on that. The thought of Monte brought Lena to his mind too vividly. He ached not so much with desire as rebellion. He had slept badly last night, and Clytie could have eased the tension in him. Only she hadn't. She lay there, pretending to be asleep, for a couple of hours, reeking of resentment. He was sure he had been the first to sleep, damn her.

Someone knocked at the door. "Come in," he shouted. It was Dr. Lavoey, to say that the funeral would be at ten-thirty tomorrow, and that Judge Dilham was grateful and touched by Downey's thoughtfulness in having the grave dug. Downey waved the doctor away impatiently.

"I figger it's my duty. I never was close enough to Roy for us to spit in each other's fireplaces, but he's a good man and it was my duty."

The doctor departed. Almost at once there was another knock. Again Downey shouted, "Come in."

A stranger opened the door diffidently and stepped inside. It was a man about his own height, but heavier, wider, and no more than thirty-three or so. He was dressed in a gray suit that had cost a fortune, and wore a fine derby hat and a silk scarf and ruffled white shirt.

"I'm looking for Sheriff Rodgerson E. Downey," he said.

"That's me. What can I do for you?"

The stranger closed the door and came over to the desk. Downey leaned back in his chair, the better to see his visitor's face. The man looked oddly familiar, with a broad face set off by short, stylish side-whiskers of a sleek, dark brown. Brown eyes and big, strong, healthy teeth. Square chin, no mustache.

The stranger put his knuckles on the desk and leaned down to smile at Downey. "Remember me, sir?" he said softly.

Downey smiled back a little uncertainly. "You look like somebody I ort to know, but dogged if I can put a name to you."

The stranger smiled more widely. "All right if I light the lamp?"

"Do it myself, sir."

Downey struck a match while the stranger removed the chimney and then replaced it and adjusted the wick. He laughed merrily at the perplexed look on Downey's face as he picked up the lamp.

"Still don't place me?"

"Afraid not," Downey said shortly. He was getting a little tired of this, and just a touch uneasy.

"Suppose I tell you what the E in your name stands for."

"It don't stand for nothing. My folks never gave me no middle name. I just stuck that letter in."

"No, your name is Edmund."

"God*damn!*" Downey exclaimed.

"I'm not going to tell anybody. Come here and indulge me a moment, sir. Let me show you something."

The stranger crossed the room to the mirror on the wall, carrying the lamp. The sheriff followed him. The stranger ranged himself beside Downey. They met each other's eyes in the mirror.

"What's this about you being a candidate for lieutenant governor, Sheriff?"

"Why do you want to know?" The sheriff was more uneasy still. "What's it to you?"

"I would be extremely proud. Look!"

The stranger lifted the lamp and Downey saw, in the lamp, his own face and one so like it that his skin shivered all up and down his back. Take off thirty years and some of that muscle and weight, put that fellow in old wore-out working clothes, and there was himself, staring back at him.

"Jesus Christ!"

He jerked his head around to stare the stranger straight in the face. Most of the resemblance vanished, but part of it remained.

"Know me now?"

"Why—why, you're Bobby's boy. She's your mother, ain't she? You're Bobby's son!" Downey choked.

"And yours."

The next thing Downey knew, the stranger had him by the arm and was supporting him back to his chair. The whole room had gone dark, and he had felt his knees buckle. The stranger—if stranger he was!—put the lamp on the desk, to use both hands to help Downey into the chair. All Downey could do was look up, gaping like a fish in warm, shallow water, trying to get his breath.

"I be dadblamed!" he managed to say at last. "Pull up a chair, why don't you. This is mighty strange, mighty strange! What does your mother call you?"

The stranger who was his son sat down, took out his wallet, and selected a card. He handed it to Downey, who read, *Edmund D. Rodgerson, Attorney at Law,* with addresses in both Omaha and Kansas City.

"We have always used Mother's maiden name, you know. The D stands for Downey."

Downey let the card fall on his desk. "I be dadblamed. How is Bobby? Your mother, I mean."

"She's not as young as she once was, but she keeps busy and well, and she enjoys life."

"She never married again?"

"How could she? She was never divorced from you."

"The hell she wasn't! Old Seal wrote to me that she was. You ask that old bastard."

"Grandfather is dead. No, there was a marriage between you and my mother, and she did not divorce you. You could not divorce her without serving her, and she was never served."

"I'm married again."

"I'm afraid it isn't a legal marriage."

"How'd you hear about me?"

"I looked you up a long time ago. Mother doesn't know that, but I did. You had just been elected sheriff here. I thought it over a long time before deciding not to raise ghosts of the past for either of us. I wish I could have known my father, but many a boy has to grow up without a father, and what I learned about you filled me with pride.

"I would not have come here now, except that Mother is considering claiming her marital rights. I don't know how good a case she would have, as a matter of law, but she has always been sentimental about you. She blames her family, as you do, for what happened. When she heard that you were going to run for lieutenant governor—"

"Where in the *hell* would she hear that?"

"Why, from Jerry Follansbee. Mother has been staying at the Fifty-one, in Curtin, and I came out to see her a week and a half ago. When Follansbee—"

"Hold it! You mean Bobby has been living at Lord Dunconan's place?"

"Yes. Lady Dunconan is a dear friend of hers."

"God*damn!* Did you happen to know the Honorable Phyllis what-the-hell-ever her name is?"

"Schoolfield is the family name." Downey's son chuckled. "They've been trying to arrange a marriage between Phyllis and me for years. Two things were lacking. First, Mother and I are a million short in cash. Second, I can't stand Phyllis."

Downey's nerves had stopped twitching, and he was as keen as a stalking puma. He leaned back, making the spring in his swivel chair squall, and marveled at this fellow who claimed to be his son. It was like looking in a mirror and seeing what you would have been, had one card fallen right here and there. Certainly this Edmund D. Rodgerson had never had to slink from anybody.

"How long you figger to be around here?"

"I don't know. I got in on the early freight this morning. I told Mother I would see you, talk to you, find out what I could, and stop and see her on my way back to Omaha. I don't know whether she'll take my advice or not, Sheriff, and I don't know what I'll advise her to do. I don't want to rake up old bones. I talked to Mother's surviving uncles—"

"That'd be Sam and Lynch Rodgerson. I never knowed them to tell the truth in their lives."

"I never knew them to lie. They told me you were happy to take a hundred dollars, as your price for getting out of St. Joe. I'm not your judge. You were very young. You had no education, no family background—"

"You can stop right there. I never seen anything about the Rodgersons that the Downeys had to take off their hats to, and my own mother was a Rodgerson."

His son waved the argument aside. He said earnestly, "I have never had, I do not have now, any ill feeling toward you. Seal, Sam, Lynch—they're all dead. They were lonely men, bitter, too ambitious. Seal—my grandfather—was the only one who ever married. Mother inherited everything they had in both Sedalia and St. Joseph. It was . . . considerable. If you and she reconcile, you would never have to worry about money again."

"I don't worry about it now. I just don't see what your mother wants to go and prod things for now."

"I'll be frank. She has never gotten over you. I doubt that she could possibly be happy in a town like this, as the wife of a country sheriff. But if you're going to be lieutenant governor, and possibly governor after that, I think perhaps she feels that it would make up for all the years you have ignored her. An abandoned wife—"

"I didn't abandon her. Her own goddamn people ran me to hell out of St. Joe at gunpoint. I didn't even know she was knocked up. And now—why, my lord, boy, I can't even remember what Bobby looks like!"

"I brought this photograph of her for you. It was taken in Omaha just last summer."

Downey stared long and hard at the picture, which was postcard-size. He tried to see in the buxom, strong-faced woman someone he remembered, someone whose body he remembered intimately, someone who had taken him to the peak of happiness and then greased the skids to hell for him. He saw nothing but a buxom, strong-faced woman with the mean eyes old Seal Rodgerson had had.

"She has got to be an old woman, ain't she?"

"Well, you're fifty-five yourself. I went to the trouble of looking you up. A man likes to know about his father. Don't you want to keep the picture?"

"No." Downey had dropped the photograph on the desk, face down. His son picked it up.

"Very well, let's both think about this. I'm due in court in Omaha next week on a very important case. I'll be back in Curtin for Christmas with Lord Dunconan. Perhaps we can talk about it then."

"You're all-fired bossy, you know that? You're going to decide what I'm going to do, is that it?"

"By no means. I have to think of Mother, but I have a

stake in this, too. I'm a Rodgerson. I'm not sure it would pay me to become a Downey, even if you were elected President."

"And if it don't pay, to hell with it. You don't have to tell me you're all Rodgerson!"

His son laughed heartily. "I see that there's a lot of you in me, as Mother always said. Sheriff—I'm not going to insult both of us by calling you 'Father'—there's no reason for me to remain here any longer. I'll catch the Flyer back to Curtin tonight and talk to Mother. I hope that you're not going to make any public mention of our connection until we have come to some mutual decision on it. I assure you that Mother and I won't. I would like to shake hands on that."

He did not go so far as to put out his hand, and neither did Downey. The swivel chair's spring screamed again as he leaned back and put his hands behind his head. "You just tell Bobby one thing for me, son," he said.

"What's that?"

"I ain't going to go around bragging to nobody that I'm connected with that family. Seal and Sam and Lynch shoved a shotgun up against my kidneys and run me out of town. My own mother was their cousin, but do you think she stood up for me? In a pig's ass, she did. She let that psalm-singing old hypocrite of a Seal—"

"Let's don't call names now. I've heard of men who doubled back to take care of wives and sons under worse threats. It seems to me you were easily driven away from your bride, sir."

"Listen, you—did you know Seal Rodgerson well?"

"Yes, and I didn't like him. I told him to go to hell a time or two, and made it stick. And I have always wondered why you never did, that's all."

"So have I," Downey burst out. He shot to his feet and put out his hand. "Howsomever you feel about me as a father, boy, I'd say you turned out to be one hell of a son. I wish I'd knowed you long ago."

They clasped hands. "So do I," his son said. "You're a hell

of a man, for fifty-five. The way you came to your feet—I'd
hate to tangle with you . . . Father."

"Father. Son of a bitch, me, a father! Excuse me. I've got
to wipe my eyes, and I ain't a bit ashamed."

"Neither am I, sir."

● ● ●

The office grew cool, and he got up blindly and stoked the
stove and sat down blindly again, without breaking the spell.
He was back home again, and home was Kansas City, where
his father had managed a theater. Made money at it, knew all
the great performers, set a famous table every Friday night.
And then the galloping consumption, when Downey was
eighteen. Shortly after Downey's nineteenth birthday, David
Sentous Downey—the D.S.D. known to singers and actors and
acrobats and dancers in New York and London and Brussels
and Paris—was dead.

His mother's cousin, Lynch Rodgerson, came to Kansas
City to liquidate the theater for Mama. Uncle Lynch took
too strong a hand with Rodgie, as his mother called him. One
evening he hit Rodgie across the mouth with the back of his
hand, cutting his lip on his teeth, and bringing blood. Never
in his nineteen years had Rodgerson Edmund Downey been
struck by another human being. He called cousin Lynch a son
of a bitch and started running. Before he got his wits back, he
was on a Missouri Pacific train with no baggage and very little
money.

A year later, thin, filthy, almost naked, and in a state of
shock from the hard buffeting life had given him, he came
back to Kansas City. The family house had been sold. A
neighbor gave him his mother's address in Sedalia. Downey—
no longer fit to be called "Rodgie"—walked every step of the
way. He never could remember what he ate or where he slept.

Sedalia was over its brief career as the twin to Dodge City
as an outlet for Texas longhorns, but it was still a very tough
town, and he wondered what in the world Mama was doing

there. Someone told him that she had sold a house that had belonged to his father, and had moved to St. Joseph to be with her family. Back to Kansas City went young Downey, and then down the Missouri as a stowaway on a cattle barge to St. Louis.

Downey's father's last words had been quoted to him often enough by cousin Lynch, as an example of vile, quarrelsome, unrepentant sinfulness, for him never to forget them: "I'm reconciled, you know, to going straight to hell. It's a comfort to know that, under no circumstances consistent with Revealed Truth, will I encounter a single, saintly, goddamn Rodgerson hypocrite, may their balls explode in Heaven."

Downey felt the same way about cousin Lynch, but he had no other place to go. He was a frightened, defeated wraith, a mama's boy to whom the whole world had turned out to be the enemy. But, to his surprise, after his mother had fainted with delight, cousin Lynch began blubbering tears of happiness as he enfolded Downey in his arms. Cousin Seal, the eldest, and the only married one, bunched his knuckles in his beard and declaimed a prayer. Sam, the youngest, the cross-eyed one, merely smiled like a fox and muttered endearments.

Seal's wife, a defeated wraith herself, did not venture an opinion. It remained for Robyna, daughter of Seal and Selma, to tender the ultimate courtesies of the clan. Bobby, as she was called, crept up the stairs to his attic room, barefoot, on his second night there. In her flannel nightgown, she looked like a ghost to him.

Fortunately, he did not scream. He was then still celibate, not out of conviction but out of poverty. The only women he had known wanted to be paid, and he had not even been able to keep himself clothed.

Meek, unsuccessful, living a life of terror after his year on his own, he obeyed her like a flunky. Bobby was a matronly woman of twenty-one, outweighing Downey by ten pounds. She initiated him into the delights of adulthood with skill and muscular ferocity.

He was there almost a year, gaining weight because he ate well but looking haggard because he slept hardly at all. When Bobby did not visit him, apprehension that she would made him restless. Not until he was much, much older did he learn to take pride in never having failed her. At the time, he was simply afraid to.

The cousins bought him new, fine clothes, and a good horse, saddle, and bridle. They owned some river barges and some riverside land, where they fattened cattle for the market. The only work he ever had to do was helping sort out cattle and drive them onto the barges for shipment. An old black man from Texas who worked for the cousins taught him to ride and rope, taught him horse sense and cattle sense, and gave him a trade.

The end came on a Sunday morning soon after his twentieth birthday. The others were finishing breakfast when Bobby came down. She looked pale and nervous as she bowed her head for the silent prayer that was the rule for all latecomers to meals. Cousin Selma handed her a plate heaped with grits, gravy, fried eggs, and side-meat.

Bobby gave a hoarse shriek and ran for the kitchen. She was too late. She could not throw up much, having spent the last hour throwing up in her bedroom, but what was left in her was sprayed all over the kitchen. Downey had never heard of "morning sickness."

"She et all that popcorn last night, you know," he said. "She has had a mighty craving for things lately, if you've noticed."

His mother burst into tears. Cousin Seal looked ready to choke to death. Cousin Selma had run into the kitchen. They could all hear Bobby whooping and sobbing and gagging in her mother's arms.

"Eddie, perhaps you should excuse yourself," Downey's mother finally said.

He did as he was told because he always did. No one stopped him as he saddled up and rode away. Perhaps it was a hunch that kept him away all that day. He always had pocket money, and he bought cheese and bologna at a country store for his midday meal.

It was the horse's idea to go home at night. Downey dismounted at the barn door. It opened in his face. A lantern glimmered, and something crashed into his jaw. He heard cousin Sam yell, "Catch the horse," as he slid to the ground and into darkness. The next thing he knew, someone was kicking him in ribs that were already in agony. He passed out again.

When he came to, cousin Lynch had him at the horse tank, and was drenching him with cold water. He hurt so much he wanted to die. He could hear cousin Seal sobbing and growling, and cousin Sam trying to reason with him.

"You only blacken your own soul with curses. The honor of the family comes before private vengeance. This little bastard has got to make an honest woman of Robyna, and then sign them papers," Sam was saying.

"Then I'm going to put my knife to him, so he'll never ruin another innocent girl!"

"No, you ain't, Seal. It happened in his own bed. Bobby went to him."

"May God strike me dead if I let you talk that way about her. I'm going to kill that boy!"

"Go ahead, and then plead unwritten law and see what Frank Barclay does. *He* was there before Rodgie, and Frank's a married man, and you cut him up with a horsewhip. He hates you enough to go into court and testify he had his way with her. He told me she's got a purple birthmark halfway between her bellybutton and her crotch. How could he know that if he didn't have her naked? How do you think a jury is going to take unwritten law then?"

A Rodgerson was able to stir them out at the courthouse to get a license that very night. Robyna became Mrs. Rodgerson Edmund Downey in a stark ceremony presided over by an untidy little preacher who seemed to be a sort of house chaplain.

Cousins Sam and Lynch signed as witnesses. Bobby, weeping, started to hurl herself into her husband's arms. Cousin Seal pried her loose.

"Go on home with your mother, Robyna. We'll be along shortly," he said.

Downey's mother (also weeping) gave him a big, wet kiss on his black-and-blue forehead before going with Bobby. Cousin Sam told Brother Brodie, the preacher, that he could run along, they'd lock up the church. The reverend one departed. The altar of the church was a plain wooden table. Cousin Lynch methodically laid out several folded papers on it. He wet an indelible pencil with his tongue and handed it to Downey.

"Sign here, Eddie—your full name, Rodgerson Edmund Downey. Now here. Now here. Now here. That does it. Bring the lantern, Sam. Seal, you go get his horse," he said when Downey had signed.

When they came out, Seal had both the horse and his twelve-gauge shotgun. He was frothing at the mouth, but Lynch retained command. He let Seal shove the muzzle of the gun into Downey's back.

"You pull that trigger, Seal, and we won't lift a hand to keep you out of the pen," he said. "Here, Eddie, is sixty-five dollars, all there was in the house. You p'int your nose west and keep riding until it'll take a month for a letter to get here. A year from today, write and let me know where you are, and I'll send you a bank draft for a hundred and thirty-five dollars. Two hundred total, about a hundred times what you're worth."

"I ain't going nowhere without my new clothes," Downey said. He did not feel brave, just stubborn, and so sore that he could count twenty or thirty separate painful places.

"I'll kill him," Seal sobbed. He leaned harder on the gun, but he did not press the trigger even when Downey reached back and shoved it aside.

"You try to point that at me again, you might as well pull

the trigger, because I'm going to hit you right in your god-damn mean old face," he said.

"Ingrate, ingrate," Seal said. "Whoremonger and wastrel and despoiler. That I should live to see the day!"

He pointed the gun at the ground while cousin Sam went to fetch Downey's valise. Downey, afraid of dying but not much more than he was afraid of living, made them wait while he opened it and took inventory of his clothing. He tied the valise on behind his fine new saddle. He took out the watch his mother had given him recently and saw that it was just two minutes past midnight.

"A new day and a new life for me! Screw every dirty Rodg-erson in the world," he said; and rode off.

It was months before he had to sell his horse, to eat. He wrote promptly on the first anniversary of his wedding, from a penny-ante ranch on the Rattlesnake River in Kiowa County, Kansas. A man had to be really broke to work there. A couple of months later he received a fat brown envelope from cousin Lynch.

In it was a draft for $135, and some papers that made no sense to him. He quit his job and rode on. In Dodge City he paid a lawyer three dollars to explain them.

"This one seems to be a judgment of the Buchanan County court, State of Missouri, conferring on you, as a married man, emancipation, and conceding your right to make contracts. Had you been recently married?" the lawyer asked.

"Well, yes."

"Apparently you petitioned the court for emancipation. This one is a bill of sale, dated the same day, in which you bargain, sell, transfer, and convey to Nellie Jane Downey, before her marriage Nellie Jane Rodgerson—"

"That's my mother."

"Yes. You sold all right, title, and interest in the estate of your father, for two hundred dollars cash."

"I did?"

"Yes. This appears to be a decree of divorce granted

Robyna Rodgerson Downey. This last one is your last will and testament, or a copy thereof, in which you leave everything of which you die possessed to any issue of your marriage with Robyna and so forth. Did you have any children?"

"No. Listen, what does all this mean?"

"Were you in love with your wife?"

Downey thought it over. "No. I didn't even like her very well."

"Well then, what this means is that you're well out of it—unless your father left a substantial estate."

Downey had not even known what an estate was.

CHAPTER 11

He sat in the office for a long, long time. Memories! It came to him that he had been what livestock men call a "slow grower." Kept a baby too long by his mother, frightened too badly by that runaway year after his father's death, and then too much kicked out of him the night of his wedding, by cousin Seal's hard boots.

Yet in all the mean, miserable years since then, he had been learning, without really understanding what it was he was learning. He had come at last to the point where an offhand chat with a stranger could awaken him to the political value of his name. That, you might say, had been the date of his rebirth.

He left a note for Monte Barrett: "Clean this goddamn office up," saddled up his best horse, and rode out of town. He wished he could talk everything over with Hugh Dean, but instinct told him it wouldn't be wise. Hugh was the best friend he had, but Downey sensed a streak of jealousy in him now. Hugh was all for him being lieutenant governor, but it was still a joke to him. And Downey was at the point where he did not want to be anybody's man, even Hugh's.

He gave his horse a good workout and talked to two big cattlemen, three small cattlemen, three farmers, sundry stray riders, a fix-it man in a house-wagon. To all he brought two terse messages. The first was that he was being pressingly importuned to run for lieutenant governor. The second was that the funeral of Judge Dilham's wife would be at ten-thirty tomorrow, and that they owed the judge a turnout.

The judge's praise of him moved him deeply whenever he

thought of it, which was fairly often. He barely knew the judge. He knew so little about political etiquette that only instinct had prevented him from addressing Dilham as "Your Honor" on the street. Dilham's approval was like a sign in the sky, to be understood much later, if at all, but to be acted on at once.

He put his horse up in the courthouse stables after dark and walked wearily home. When he opened his front door a cloud of steam assailed him. In the kitchen, the top of the stove was red-hot under the wash boiler. Clytie was scrubbing away at the kitchen table with a stiff brush and a pail of suds. She was back in overalls, but barefoot, and she had a rag tied around her hair.

On a chair in a corner sat Charley Noble, eating one hard-boiled egg after another from a bowl on another chair.

"This dratted hard water!" Clytie said. "Nothing comes clean."

Charley said nothing, but he got to his feet, with his mouth open, full of egg. Downey walked past both of them to the stove. An old broomstick leaned on end in the wash boiler. He used it to prod around in the vessel, bringing up some of his own underwear, some dish towels, and two suits of Charley Noble's underwear.

He rammed the broomstick back into the mess of boiling clothes. "How long do you aim to be tearing around here tonight?" he asked Clytie.

"I don't know. What I don't do tonight will have to be done tomorrow, so I might as well finish it."

"No use trying to sleep down here, then. I'll go upstairs again."

Charley went to the water pail and swigged down a dipper of water, disposing of the eggs. "Reckon I'll turn in too," he said. "Goodnight."

His door closed behind him. Downey and Clytie stood looking at each other for a moment. Clytie narrowed her eyes.

"Someday," she said softly, "you'll come back to my bed and find I ain't there."

"Come on to bed now. Come in and lock the door. Or come upstairs with me."

He thought she was going to cry. "Not tonight. I don't mean to pick a fight with you."

He did not answer. Going up the steps reminded him of the stairs to the attic that Bobby had climbed so often, so very long ago. Briefly, he felt he was actually in the attic bedroom again, and Bobby was inside the door, closing it, hurrying barefoot to assume command of the bed like a new foreman.

He lighted the lamp and held it up to look about him. Besides the narrow bed and a small bureau they had bought when two of Clytie's younger brothers lived with them to go to school, the attic contained nothing but boxes and kegs and packages of dubious properties. There was considerable doubt that what he sought had survived the attrition of the years, but if it had—

He found it in the third wooden box, with some other mementos of the hard, early years before he went to work for Hugh Dean. He untied the twine around the old brown envelope carefully. Carefully, he removed the bundle of papers inside.

They were as good as new, and the decree of divorce was on top. And that, he thought, is that. . . . Bobby could no longer do as she pleased about claiming her marital rights. Here was the proof that he had been a single man when he married Clytie. He could use it or not use it, as he chose.

He shuffled through the other papers, understanding them better now. He wondered just how much his father had been worth when he died. The way he remembered things, it would seem that cousin Lynch had made a bad error in judgment. The way he had treated Downey at first, when he came to Kansas City to settle the estate, indicated that Lynch had not thought it amounted to much.

But he must have changed his mind after Downey ran away. It had been worth fighting over, that was sure, or he would not have been welcomed to St. Joe that way. Nor would Bobby have made so free with those attic stairs, either. Cousin Seal *had* to know what she was doing. His excess of morality after Bobby puked all over everything and gave herself away showed a guilty conscience. The damned old hypocrite had baited the trap with his own daughter, no doubt aware that if Downey didn't get her pregnant, somebody would who didn't have an estate worth stealing.

Downey rolled and smoked one cigarette, and then stretched out on the narrow attic bed and slept the sleep of the just. He awakened at four, as usual, and had coffee boiling when Charley Noble came out. Downey forced a smile.

"I was going to fry up some eggs, Charley. Want I should fry three or four for you?"

Charley was a little nervous, but he agreed. They breakfasted in sociable silence, letting Clytie sleep after what probably had been a long, hard night of work. She had no sense when she got a cleaning fit.

"I got to go to Mrs. Dilham's funeral today, and I need a bath and a shave," Downey said.

"I'll shave you while the boiler is heating up. It won't take long to get bath water. It don't cool off that much overnight," Charley said, too eagerly.

Downey's nerves, which had relaxed a bit while he slept, came taut again. He could hear the early-morning freight whistling for the crossing a mile and a half east of town. The damn thing wasn't going to be as late as it usually was, and Jerome Follansbee was supposed to be on it. He stood up.

"See you at your shop in forty minutes or so, how's that, Charley?"

"I'll be waiting for you, Mr. Downey."

Downey hastened down the hill. Winter was going to hold off a little longer. It had warmed up, yet without the threat of rain that a warm streak so often meant at this time of year.

At the station, the train had stopped with the caboose at the platform, and Follansbee was just descending the steps. He looked spry and wide awake for so old a man, and he smiled in friendly fashion as he recognized Downey. They shook hands, and Follansbee confessed that he had not had breakfast and was ravenously hungry. Downey promised to take him to Tong Ti's, where he could eat in a private room and shave while it was being prepared, if he liked. The banker was considerably flattered by so much obsequious attention.

"Well, this has to be kept kind of secret, as you prob'ly can understand. We have shoved our stack into a pretty big game," Downey said nervously.

"We have indeed. Catching Chesty Bob before he can even attempt his master stroke would be wonderful."

They were leaving the platform, arm in arm, when the station agent hurried past them, bearing a telegram in his hand. Downey put his fingers in his mouth and pealed a blasting whistle that stopped the agent in his tracks.

"Who is that for, at this hour?"

"Why, I reckon it's all right to tell you. It's for Ben Chase, and it's marked 'urgent.'"

"You going to take it to his house?"

"Sure. You have to, with an urgent one."

"I'll want to see a copy of that later."

The agent shook his head. "I couldn't do that, Sheriff. You'd get me fired from my job sure."

Downey gave him a malevolent look that warned him that they would discuss this again. He took Follansbee to Tong Ti's and had him installed in the room where he and Louie Varden had eaten. He made Follansbee promise to stay out of sight until he came for him.

He hurried toward the De Luxe. Passing the Hillary Hotel, he was hailed by the night desk clerk. "A guest left this for you before boarding the Flyer for the East last night, Sheriff," he said. "He told me no hurry, or I'd've sent it over last night."

Downey opened it and read:

R. E. Downey, Esq.
Dear Sir:

While this may be too formal considering our relationship, I do not feel I can presume to do otherwise. I have had the opportunity to learn what high esteem you hold in the public mind here. Your constituents speak of you respectfully and in some cases fondly. With a little attention to personal appearance, you would reflect dignity on an otherwise nincompoop state office, if your aspirations continue to take you in that direction.

More important, I detect in you a strong will that I believe is one of my own traits. Whether it is for good or evil remains to be seen, but I believe you will not be denied in anything you set your heart on. I take a great deal of personal pride in that trait, which helps me to understand myself better.

I shall report to our mutual connection all I have learned. She will make her own decision, which I will of course support. I may, I hope, tender not merely my respect, but my warm affection as well. It has been a most rewarding visit, and I remain,

Your dutiful servant,

E. D. R.

"So Bobby will make her own decision, will she? We'll see about that! But if he is my son—and I reckon he sure enough is—I'm proud of him," Downey muttered.

"How's that?"

Downey realized that he had been speaking aloud, and that the hotel clerk was waiting as though for orders. "Nothing, nothing," he said.

"Anything I can do for you, Sheriff?"

"No, I reckon not. Yes, there is. I need a couple of water glasses, two that ain't the same kind. Have you got any to spare in the hotel?"

The clerk did. He brought one plain one and one of brown glass. Downey thanked him and hurried with the glasses to the barber shop. It was unlocked. As he opened the door, he knew he was beginning a dangerous showdown act. His whole life hung on its outcome, yet he was completely cool. All his life he had dreaded crises, had cowered before them, had had to nerve himself or be driven to them. But he walked into this one with excitement rather than dread, and with a perfect willingness to stake all on his own judgment.

Charley had lighted the two big lamps that illuminated the chair. He had finished shaving himself and was mopping away the last lather with a hot, wet towel. Downey held up the two glasses and winked. Charley broke into a big, silly, horse-toothed grin.

"Well, say! I'd forgot about them. Want a little shot now, first thing?"

"No. I don't like to smell whiskey on the breath of a man leaning over me with a razor."

Charley grinned wider than ever. "Lay back in the chair, Mr. Downey, and let me practice my arts on you. It's cozy in here, ain't it? That brown glass is real pretty. That's a bunch of grapes on it, ain't it?"

"Yes. That's your glass, Charley. The plain one is mine. Plain glass for a plain man—fancy glass for a fancy dude."

Charley giggled self-consciously and began to strop his razor. Downey enjoyed nothing so much as a bought shave from a good barber, and Charley was good. He was also fast. In a twinkling, Downey was smooth of face and reeking prettily of bay rum.

"I'll have that drink now, Charley."

"Me too. It would just hit the spot."

Downey picked up the glasses. They went into the boiler room. Charley retrieved the bottle and then put it down.

"Wait a minute, Mr. Downey. I want to show you something that nobody else here knows about."

He knelt beside the kindling box that held pieces of pitch-pine, pine knots, pine cones, and excelsior. From behind it he took a wooden box with mortised corners. It was an old dynamite box, but with its lid now cleated and hinged, and locked with a hasp and padlock. Downey would have given a lot to know what was in it, but Charley closed it after making one quick grab.

"I wore this for better than three months," he said, handing Downey a United States deputy marshal's badge. "I thought I was fixed for life, but the marshal got fired, and the new one didn't want me. Want to know why I kept that, when I could've got my two dollars back on it?"

"Everybody keeps souvenirs, Charley."

"It's more than a souvenir. That's proof that once I was *somebody*. It's something to live up to. That was in the Territory of Arizona, when it was a tough old place. Of course, it wouldn't mean nothing to you. You're an old hand at it."

Downey handed the badge back. Charley babbled on as he replaced it in the box and snapped the padlock. Instantly, he became the serious host. He got out the bottle, pulled the cork. It had not been clear in Downey's mind how he was going to get the stuff into Charley's whiskey—only that, one way or another, he would.

Charley solved his problem for him. "Wait a minute, Mr. Downey," he said, and went back into the barber shop. Downey snatched the little brown bottle out, smashed the wax seal on the iron boiler, and took hold of the little wire grip on the cork. He pulled gently. The cork came out.

How much of this stuff was he supposed to slop in? Was it three drops? He could not be sure, but he certainly did not want to kill Charley. He put his thick fingertip over the mouth of the bottle, dripped in three drops, and then three more. He stoppered the bottle, put it back in his pocket, and picked up the whiskey.

He was pouring the drinks when Charley returned. He picked up the clear glass himself, to make sure that Charley got the brown one with the bunch of grapes formed in the glass, and the chloral hydrate inside. Again Charley grinned his foolish grin, as he picked up the brown glass.

"A little toast, Mr. Downey. I had to go back in the shop and get out a paper where I wrote it down, but I can say it now."

They hoisted their glasses, and Charley recited:

> "Here's to the breezes
> That blow through the trees-es
> And blow the chemises
> Above the girls' knees-es,
> And show all the boys where to get their diseases,
> B'Jesus."

"How!" Downey replied.

They tossed off their drinks. Charley said something about Downey's bath, but Downey wanted him in the shop. There was nothing Charley could do but follow Downey, who picked up a bottle from the shelf.

"Will this stuff really work, Charley?"

"It won't bring hair back to a dead scalp," Charley said, "but it'll save what's left, even if it's only the roots. Why?"

"I've often wondered. You sure sell a lot of it, don't you?"

"Yes, that's a real money-maker. I'm just dead for sleep, Mr. Downey. Guess I haven't been"—Charley yawned—"going to bed early enough."

Downey took him by the arm and guided him, backward, to his own barber chair. Charley gave a little yelp as he lost his balance, and Downey had to jump behind him to catch him before he fell. He hoisted the barber into the chair and stepped back.

Lord, lord, but that stuff worked fast! When he pinched Charley's cheek, nothing happened. Charley just lay there, breathing lightly.

Downey used Charley's own scissors to whack off, a chunk at a time, that big red mustache. He beat up a lather and used Charley's razor to shave off the stubble. A totally new man now lay in the chair.

He locked the shop behind him and strode swiftly to Tong Ti's, where Jerome Follansbee had finished breakfast. The old man walked so slowly that Downey took hold of his arm to help him along.

"Man might think I was under arrest, Mr. Downey," the banker said.

"Sorry, Mr. Follansbee."

"Quite all right, Rodge, if I may call you that. If we're going to work together, it's time to cut out the 'mister.' My name is Jerry or Rome, either one."

"Appreciate that, Rome."

They were at the shop. Downey unlocked it, held the door open, closed it behind Follansbee, and shot home the bolt. "Charley Noble" slept on in his own barber chair.

Downey stepped over to him and, with a flourish, snatched off the expensive red-brown toupee.

"Well, Rome, what do you say now?"

"Who is that?" said Follansbee.

"Why, that's Chesty Bob Nylander."

Follansbee looked shocked and horrified. "Oh dear, no— my goodness, no! As I told you, I got to know Chesty Bob very well indeed, and I have never seen that man there in my life."

CHAPTER 12

Downey did not really know what was happening around him until almost an hour later. He had felt other crushing blows in his life, but none like this. Not only would he not be elected lieutenant governor—he would be a laughing-stock who could not even win another election to sheriff. He was as good as dead.

He was sitting at his desk, his face in his hands, when Monte Barrett came in. "Ben Chase would like to see you. Him and some other feller has been looking all over for you," said Monte.

Downey raised his head. "What other feller?"

"I don't know. Some little old dried-up wart in a stiff collar. Are you sick, Mr. Downey? You look like hell."

"I feel like hell. What are you all dressed up for?"

"Mrs. Dilham's funeral, don't you remember? Lena's going, too. They're waiting at the bank, if you want to see them."

What he wanted more than anything else was to die, but a stubborn rage came to his rescue, and he picked up his hat and stumbled out of the room. In the short, dark corridor, the county assessor tried to stop him. Downey pushed blindly past him as the rage continued to rise in him.

So Follansbee hadn't been content to witness his degradation—he had to spread it all over Downey's own town, did he? People who approached Downey with the intention of speaking to him fell back from his scowl as he plodded heavily but swiftly toward the Hillary State Bank. A trio of jobless cowboys, loafing in the door of the bank, out of the chill wind, scattered like quail after beholding his face.

Follansbee sat at the end of the desk, at Ben's right hand, in the place of honor. He was talking away, thirteen to the dozen. Downey caught Lord Dunconan's name, and the rage in him became something murderous. If the damned old senile fool thought Lord Dunconan meant anything in Wyoming, he was betting a bobtail straight. Bobby's connections would be a lot better than Follansbee's.

Ben indicated a smaller chair in a less distinguished position. "Glad you could drop in, Rodge. We want to ask you just how keen you think this detective fellow is."

Downey ignored the chair, to lean his weight on the desk with both hands. "What detective? Do you mean Louie Varden?"

"Yes. Is he as good as he thinks he is?"

"Why do you want to know?"

Ben's face showed his resentment. He was dressed in his best, no doubt for the funeral, and hearing Lord Dunconan's name used so familiarly by a caller at his bank had given him a double shot of self-esteem.

"I don't think I like your tone of voice, Rodge."

"And I don't care whether you like it or not. You got a telegram this morning. I want to see it."

"I got two, as a matter of fact, but I don't know what gives you the idea that you can—"

"Show him the one from Varden, for pity's sake," Follansbee interjected. "We need Rodge's help, Ben. I trust him implicitly. He has already eliminated one false trail in his pursuit. I can testify to that personally."

Downey spared a quick glance at Follansbee. The old fool was batting his eyes and smiling like a 'possum, a look that made them coconspirators. He had not, after all, blabbed his brains out about Charley Noble. To Follansbee, that had been merely an incident in a busy sheriff's life.

Downey made a lightning readjustment. He could have

wept with gratitude, but he knew that any premature celebration was dangerous. He was still on thin ice, and his best defense was still to be as offensive as he could. He pointed a thick, trembling finger at Ben.

"Ben, listen, I've got a lot on my mind today, but I'm trying to be patient with you. For Christ's sake, either come to the point or don't bother me."

Ben took two folded telegrams out of his vest pocket. He glanced at them, folded one and put it back in the pocket, and handed the other to Downey. It said:

URGE YOU TAKE EXTREMELY SERIOUSLY TIP THAT EFFORT WILL BE MADE THIS TIME SURE STOP ALL PRECAUTIONS PRIOR SHIPMENT MUST REPEAT MUST BE TAKEN STOP CUSTODY NOT OURS UNTIL RECEIPT SIGNED STOP REQUEST YOUR FRIENDLY INTERCESSION WHEN I AM PROVED RIGHT.

It was signed by Louie Varden. No use asking when "this time" was. What this wire meant was that the banks had already been given, by coded wire, a date for the money train. Varden, who took his mysterious tips very seriously indeed, was not going to get off his rump to shoot it out with Chesty Bob or anybody else. No, sir, all he was going to do was sit there and fire off wires to try to get his hands on part of the reward.

Downey dropped the long-winded telegram on the desk. He leaned over and plucked the other one out of Ben Chase's vest pocket. Ben gave a sharp yelp of surprise and anger, but Downey was already reading:

MEETING OPENED WITH PRAYER AND BUGLE SOLO
O. F. LOUIS

"Let's see the code." Downey snapped his fingers. "Come on, Ben—the code, the code!"

"The—the code?"

"Shit, Ben. Whose idee do you think this code was?"

"But we were all sworn to secrecy."

"Nothing," said Jerome Follansbee, "seems to be secret to Rodge. I declare, Ben, this man is half tiger, half bloodhound."

Ben got an envelope out of his desk and handed it over. The top and bottom lines were, *Destroy At Once on Receipt of Telegraphic Schedule.* Downey looked down the brief column of coded words. "Bugle" meant "one" and "meeting" meant "eastbound."

He handed the card back. "Tomorrow. I don't know what good it is to set up a code system, Ben, if you're too damn dumb to read. You're supposed to tear that up the minute you get the wire."

"Well, this is the first time we've used the system," Chase said. He began shredding the card. Downey put out his hand, and Chase dropped the bits of cardboard into it.

"I am inclined to take this warning seriously, Rodge," Follansbee said. "The lady I mentioned in our private conversation—know who I mean?"

"Sure." He meant the Honorable Phyllis. Downey pulled the ashtray across the desk and carefully set fire to the pieces of cardboard in it. "If you're going to have a secret code, Ben, keep it secret."

Follansbee went on, "She said that this man is obsessed with train-robbing. He had only contempt for the Jennings Brothers, for instance, but great admiration for the Daltons. He said that Jesse James would have been governor of Missouri if he had stuck to trains instead of banks. He knows of train robbers and robberies that I have never heard of. Some names new to me were Swingle, McNutt, Big Buck Fanchon —do these mean anything to you?"

"Sure, sure, but the important thing is, how much money have you two got at stake tomorrow? Ben, how much are you shipping, or are you getting some in?"

"Neither."

"How much cash in the vault?"

"This is an outrage!" But Chase thought better of it, after Follansbee merely tapped him on the arm. "We have something like twenty-two thousand in the vault now. I'm holding an extra-large reserve because Hugh Dean is buying some Oklahoma yearlings and will need the cash. We have a few 'bearer' bonds, too."

"What do you call a few?"

Ben's face got pinker still. "Fifteen thousand dollars' worth." It hit him suddenly, and he stumbled to his feet. "Good God, thirty-seven thousand dollars! The governor ought to put militia on that train. Why doesn't he? I'm going to wire him and demand that he do so!"

"You do," Downey said, "and every saloon bum along the UP will know that there's a rich money train coming through, and that your bank is hog-fat with cash, and that Chesty Bob is going to clean us out like a duck eating mulberries. Know what you ort to do? You ort to call Hugh Dean and tell him to come get his goddamn money and take care of it himself. Let him take care of yours, too, while he's at it. Send a man out now."

"That's the most ridiculous thing I ever heard. Oh dear, what am I going to do?"

"Nothing. What have you got a sheriff for?"

"Oh shoot, Rodge, this is too much for you!"

"It is?" Downey leaned over the desk to glare red-eyed at Chase. "You thought you was pretty cute, you and Louie Varden, trying to fool me with that code—me! I knowed about it before you did, didn't I?"

"Yes, but—"

"Get your cash out of the bank, or take your losses. Jerry, you better get back to Curtin and take care of your own money, just in case. And let me worry about Chesty Bob and the Union Pacific."

His feeling of desolation returned briefly, after he had left the bank. He clamped his jaws shut and refused to give in to it. His back might be against the wall, but they still had him to deal with. His big worry was Louie Varden and his inside information. No matter how great Varden's fame as a detective, Downey had little respect for him. Louie was slick. He was a man who made everything he said sound important, and he *looked* like a cool-nerved, crafty sleuth. But Downey was sure he was a bluffer and conniver who had gotten where he was by taking credit for other men's work. Just as he had planned to cash in on the rewards for Chesty Bob.

But even a bluffer and conniver could pick up information that was reliable. Nor did Downey put too much trust in the code system, especially on its trial run. He had a hunch that Chesty Bob's information on the money-train's schedule was better than Varden's on Chesty Bob.

Didn't that add up to a stickup tomorrow? If Chesty Bob was dying to hold up a train, as Lady Phyllis said, could there be a better time? But why here in Hillary? Hillary had made sense once, when he thought Charley Noble was Chesty Bob. But who could have done the long, careful job of preparation on the site, that had made Chesty Bob's jobs such stunning successes?

A man stopped him, daring his absent scowl. "Charley Noble ain't opened his shop yet, Sheriff," he said. "First time he's been this late. Is he sick or what?"

"Do you need a haircut or something?"

"No, but I thought—"

"I'll do the thinking in this town. Get out of my way! I'll go see if Charley's there."

The loafers who sought the barber-shop stove in this weather were lurking disconsolately near Charley's door, but they knew better than to come close when Downey unlocked it and went in. Charley was still sound asleep in his chair. He was so still that a cold streak raced through Downey, but when he put his hand on Charley's chest he could feel the rise and fall of his respiration. He tweaked Charley's cheek, saw the white spot where he had pressed, and saw it turn to Charley's normal red again. He slipped out, locking the door behind him.

"Charley's taking a nap. Reckon he don't feel so well today," he reported.

He went home and found Clytie waiting to go to the funeral in a dress of dark purple, with a black veil over her hair and face. To Downey, the veil looked seductive rather than reverent, and he was not sure about purple for a funeral. He changed quickly into his best pants, pearl-handled gun, and black Sunday hat.

The church was full to overflowing, but when the sheriff and his lady appeared, room was made for them. They went to the cemetery for the graveside commitment, Clytie weeping softly against Downey's arm. When Judge Dilham had thrown in the symbolic handful of cold dirt, the two men Downey had hired stepped forward with their shovels. They looked at him expectantly, but he shook his head.

"After the job is finished," he said out of the corner of his mouth.

A small crowd separated itself from the departing mourners to surround the judge, but he insisted on coming to Downey's side. "Thank you so much for telling people about the services, Rodge," he said. "I heard of your long ride about the county yesterday."

"Well, Judge, people want to know when somebody as nice as your wife passes on. They got a right to know. That's part of my job."

"I would like to ask you to my house for a few minutes, if you have time."

Clytie excused herself to return to her household duties. The judge, taking hold of Downey's arm, watched her swaying down the path in her purple dress, trailing in the fall wind the veil that was tied about her hair and face. But he did not speak until they had reached his house, and Downey, impatiently, had cleaned the ashes from both stoves and carried them out to the pile.

"You will never see your wife grow old," the judge said, as Downey sat down after stirring up the fire.

The sheriff had to think hard to phrase what was in his mind. He cleared his throat. "I just found out that I've got a son by my first marriage."

"Well! Have you two met?"

"Yes. He—he's a hell of a man, Judge."

"How does he feel about you, do you think?"

"I reckon he's proud. He said so, and he don't strike me as somebody that would crap you about it."

"Well, Rodge, I knew there was more about you than Hugh Dean ever saw in you. Your wisdom and humility come from great suffering and great sorrow, and I have sensed that all along."

"Judge, I ain't wise and I ain't humble. I—sometimes I'm so ambitious that I wonder where the hell I got the nerve. Me —me, that's been whipped out of town with a rope with a knot in the end, like a stray dog. I reckon I was the no-accountest kid that—"

There was a loud drumming on the door, and the voices of excited boys competing to detail some direly exciting news. Downey leaped up to answer, to save the judge the effort. He knew all three boys. They were eleven or twelve years old, and completely agog.

"Monte Barrett wants you to come quick," said one. "Some goddamn tramp cowboy is fixing to shoot up the town."

"Watch your language! I hear you talking like that again, I'll whip your hind end myself." Downey reached for his hat. "I wish I had my everyday gun on. I'd hate to kill anybody with this one."

"Have you killed anyone with the other one?"

"No, come to think of it, I haven't."

"Thank your wife for the food she brought over earlier. Roasted ribs of beef, potatoes baked with cheese and bacon bits, fresh bread, wild strawberry jam—she's a wonder, Rodge! But I'm sure you know that."

CHAPTER 13

He heard two screaming bullets and the gunshots that went with them, and knew that the sport who was having his fun with this town was using a rifle. By the time he got to the street, it was deserted. The moment he stepped into it, near Erik Sontag's store, a bullet shrieked past him. It missed him by a foot, but a foot was too close. A foot made it personal.

The fool was down there near Charley Noble's barber shop somewhere. Downey did not have to ponder this conclusion. He backtracked and raced down an alley for two and a half long blocks. The back door of the Hillary Hotel was locked, but a frightened Indian girl who worked as a housemaid opened it for him.

"It's Joe Ogren, and he's crazy drunk. He almost hit me," she squeaked.

"Don't you worry, Bessie. We'll put an ax handle between his spokes," he comforted her.

He went to the lobby of the hotel, to where he could see across the street and down half a block. The big, clumsy cowboy was leaning against Charley's very door as he reloaded the rifle. A .45 swung in a holster on his flank, and when he had filled the magazine of the rifle, he reloaded the pistol. The plank sidewalk around him had a dozen twinkling brass empties on it.

"Can you hit him from a window upstairs?" came the whisper of the maid, Bessie.

"Hit him? Oh, shoot, that ain't the way to tame these wild cowboys. You stay out of the way and don't try to learn me how to suck eggs."

She watched him adoringly as he returned to the alley through the same back door. He would have to take the long way around, and there was no time to go on foot. He hoped that there was a good horse in the hotel's stable. There usually was.

There was this time. He threw somebody's saddle and bridle on somebody's nimble little gray mare, led her down the alley to the end, and mounted her. She ran like a rabbit across weedy lots until he knew it was safe to come out on the road. He crossed it to the railroad right-of-way and turned back in the other direction. At the depot, he tied the horse securely and gave it a grateful and admiring slap on the rump.

"Good horse! Wish I owned you."

He could hear more gunfire, and the crash and tinkle of glass, as he sprinted to the courthouse. Monte Barrett saw him coming and came out to meet him.

"Did the Cooke kid find you, Mr. Downey?"

"I'm here, ain't I?"

"I didn't want to get into no shooting match without orders. He ain't hit nobody yet, but—"

"What's he sore about this time?"

"He wants a haircut and a shave, and Charley hasn't opened up yet. If we come at him from both ends of the block, one of us is bound to—"

"Monte, what do you want to do, kill this poor deluded fool? You come with me and learn something."

He did not stop to borrow a key to unlock the gate behind Sontag's store this time. That fool was whanging away with his .45 now, and couldn't have heard a horse running over him. Downey raised a foot and rammed his boot heel against the gate. It held, but he heard the squeak of nails yielding. He nodded to Monte, and they kicked at the same time, and kicked again.

The gate yielded in the middle, leaving a post dangling in the chain. Downey ran on tiptoe to the door of the boiler room. It had to be opened forcibly, too, but they had to wait a moment while Joe Ogren reloaded. Downey could hear him grumbling loudly to himself as he did so, cursing an ungrateful town that locked its doors against an honest working man.

Joe began shooting again. Charley's door yielded to a single kick, and Downey led the way through the bath house and into the shop. Monte drew in his breath sharply when he beheld Charley asleep in his chair. Downey felt a chill himself, to see Charley sleeping through Ogren's fusillade. Monte would have stopped to give aid to Charley, but Downey shook his head angrily.

He had to fiddle with his key to unlock the door, and when the tongue of the latch retracted, it did so with a hearty click. Ogren turned with the .45 in his hand as Downey yanked the door back. Downey leaped at him, remembering to push the gun-arm *upward*, and not downward against Ogren's best strength.

The gun went off in his face. He felt the sting of burning powder, the muzzle-glare blinded him, and a gust of pure power lifted his hat and sent it sailing. He drove a left fist into Ogren's stomach and tried to hook his foot behind Ogren's ankle. The cowboy was four inches the taller and twenty pounds the heavier, and a better rough-and-tumble fighter than Downey had thought he would be. He had an arm like an oak cornerpost, and pounding on his belly was like pounding on Charley's boiler.

Monte watched his chance and pushed past the two struggling men. Downey could see and feel the .45 as it came around to center on his abdomen. He got a hand on the gun and thrust it aside, just as Joe squeezed the trigger. Downey banged his forehead against Joe's face and took his teeth in the forehead.

Then Monte was on Joe's back, one arm around Joe's throat and the other hauling on his gun-arm. Downey got a leg around one of Joe's and threw his whole weight forward.

He kept hold of the barrel of Joe's gun as they toppled together, but he caught himself in time to slam a right fist at
Joe's chin as they went down.

The blow had all his weight and all his muscle behind it.
Joe went limp. Downey stood up and took Joe by the wrist to
drag him off Monte, so Monte could stand up too.

"Get his weapon, Monte, and get back out of his reach,"
he panted. "In case he comes to."

He looked around for something with which to tie Joe's
hands. He had handcuffs in the office, but he had been
handcuffed himself a time or two, and he hated the things.
The few times he had had to secure a prisoner's arms, he had
used a short length of chain and a padlock. It was incon-
venient for the arresting officer, but it did the job and was
somehow less ignominious than handcuffs—was somehow
complimentary, even.

"I couldn't get to him no quicker," Monte quavered.

"You done fine! Watch him, while I get something to tie
him up with."

"You're bleeding like a pig, Mr. Downey."

Downey could feel the sting on his forehead now, and
when he swiped his arm across it he brought it back bloody.
"Where I butted his teeth," he panted. "He must have iron
teeth, the son of a bitch. Watch him!"

He found some new, quarter-inch rope in Charley's woodshed. He bound Ogren's wrists behind him. The cowboy slept
on, reeking of yesterday's whiskey and some not-quite-so-stale
that he had drunk today.

"Once when I's about your age, Monte, I let a trick shooter
in a circus shoot pipes out of my mouth and apples off my
head. That's just how bad I needed five dollars. Ever since
then, I get sick at my stomach when a bullet comes too close
to me."

"You sure didn't act scared. You climbed him like a cinna-
mon bear, Mr. Downey. Say, what's the matter with Charley
Noble in there?"

"I don't know. You walk this chump down and throw him in jail. Don't even bother to untie him. Then you go and get Doc Lavoey as fast as you can."

"How can I walk him when—?"

Downey hauled Ogren to his feet and slapped him across the face twice. Ogren opened his eyes—and then his mouth. Downey got out of the way as Ogren threw up. Ogren struggled against his bonds a couple of times and then gave up, to glare with sullen hatred at Downey.

"You ever lay hands on me again—" he managed to choke out.

"On your way, Monte!"

Downey could see them converging on the barber shop from all sides, now that the shooting was over. He ducked inside the barber shop and locked the door, leaving the key in it. Hurrying toward the bath, he caught a glimpse of himself in one of Charley's mirrors. The blood that he had wiped across his forehead was drying there, and the lump under the one-inch gash in the skin was starting to rise and turn purple.

Well, he thought, the hell with that. . . . In the boiler room, he got out the bottle and both glasses. He took the little brown bottle of chloral hydrate from his hip pocket and emptied it into the whiskey bottle. He corked the bottle, shook it vigorously, and then poured the clear glass—his own —half full. He left glasses and bottle in plain sight.

Charley felt plenty warm to the touch, and he seemed to feel it a little when Downey pinched his cheek. But his color was bad. He was neither white nor red, but a sort of blue-gray.

Lavoey pounded on the door and Downey admitted him. While the doctor used his stethoscope, Downey told his tale.

"He had this secret bottle back there for just him and me, see, and I brought a couple of glasses from the hotel. We was going to have a drink together this morning, is all. He recited some kind of a fool poem and drank his down. I only took a sip of mine. Charley started to get limber-legged, so I put mine down and grabbed him before he could fall. It's still set-

ting there, my drink I mean. I bet that bottle is full of knockout drops."

"Let me see," Lavoey said suspiciously.

"Can you tell if it is loaded?"

"I can't. I suppose a chemist could."

"If we could try it on a dog, or something—"

"Yes, all we need is a whiskey-drinking dog."

Downey grabbed the doctor by the arm and spun him
around. "Spit it out, Jim, goddamnit. Are you saying that *I*
loaded *his* bottle?"

"You asked me, Rodge, and by God I'll tell you. I can't see
Charley doing a thing like that, but I sure wouldn't put it
past you."

The twin ghosts of guilt and fear touched their cold hands
on the back of Downey's neck. He deliberately eased the
check on his anger, driving them away. He tightened his grip
on the doctor's arm, to make it hurt.

"Man makes a statement like that," he said softly, "he better be ready to back it up."

"Let go. You're hurting me."

"I mean to hurt you. Tell you what, Jim—let's trade jobs.
I'll take care of Charley and you find out how that stuff got
into the whiskey. You'd make a hell of a policeman."

Doc gave up struggling, but he did not drop his eyes before
Downey's furious ones. "Maybe you didn't. You said a 'secret' bottle. Maybe it wasn't so secret. But, Rodge, I've seen
you cut across lots many a time, breaking the law you're supposed to enforce, and you're just too ambitious to be trusted.
Now, I hear, you're going to run for lieutenant governor."

"I'm going to run for lieutenant governor, so I slip Charley
knockout drops. Why?"

"Everybody knows Charley is sweet on your wife."

Downey slapped him. He let go of Doc's arm to do it, and
he hit him so hard that Doc sat down on the floor. He looked
up with cold hatred in his eyes, and wiped the blood from his
lips.

"What became of his mustache?" he said.

"I took it off for him. I thought the son of a bitch had tried to load a drink on me, and somehow switched the glasses. All right, I thought to myself, you're so funny, let's see how you like it. You come in here and look at this whiskey!"

He hauled Lavoey roughly to his feet and pushed him back into the boiler room. Lavoey smelled both bottle and glass, and touched his tongue to the liquor in the clear glass. He shook his head.

"You can't smell it and you can't taste it, in ordinary quantities. We'll have to get Charley on his feet and start walking him. Black coffee is the thing, as soon as we can get it down him."

"That's what I thought myself. But you're the doctor and I'm the sheriff, and I don't try to tell you your business."

"Rodge, I shot off my mouth, yes I did. I'm sorry for that, yes I am. There's something about you that always has rubbed me the wrong way, and when you take a good-looking man like Charley into your own home, and your wife is so much younger than you are—"

"You and Charley can get well together in the same bed, if you keep on."

"I apologize. I reckon I've got a big mouth." Doc scowled at the bottle and glasses again. "Who takes charge of this, you or me?"

"I want just enough of it to try on a dog. If you don't know how to drench a dog, I do."

"I want to see that, but first let's get Charley on his feet."

Downey had to manhandle the loafers who jammed the door the moment they opened it. He selected three of them to help with Charley. They got the barber on his feet and hustled him outside. Two or three breaths of cold air seemed to revive him.

"Charley, what happened?" Dr. Lavoey asked.

Charley's blue eyes remained at half-mast, but he struggled

to raise his right hand. "Here's to the breezes that blow through the trees-es," he said indistinctly. His eyes closed. He snored.

"That's what he recited when he drank his drink, Doc. He don't know where he is or what time it is or what he's doing," said Downey.

"Walk him down to Tong Ti's place and start slopping the black coffee into him. Make sure you don't burn his mouth, and keep him on his feet and walking," the doctor instructed the men who had Charley in charge. The whole parade, a dozen strong, set off down the street enthusiastically.

"It beats me," said Lavoey. "Who in the world would do that to poor, harmless Charley Noble?"

"Maybe," said Downey, "they was after me."

"If they were, you're lucky to be alive. So is Charley."

Eph Bascom's fool-hound came lolloping down the street. It was a big, rangy, powerful dog of excellent family. Its ancestors had all been good coon-dogs. Its litter mates were all good coon-dogs. Bascom had paid fifteen dollars for the pick of the litter, and it had turned out to be a genetic sport, a born fool that could not be trained to do anything but act the fool.

Downey snapped his fingers. "You come here, Fool," he said. The dog capered to him joyously. Downey took out his handkerchief (taking care not to expose the empty brown bottle still in that pocket), and made a collar of it for the dog. He held Fool while Dr. Lavoey brought the bottle.

There was a wrong way and a right way to go at these things, and the wrong way was the gentle way. Downey stood up, leaned over, and put his left arm around Fool. He lifted the dog up, squeezed him back against his own stomach, and used his right hand to pry Fool's mouth open. "Don't try to pour it in too fast. We don't want to drown the worthless thing," he said.

The doctor got the neck of the bottle between the dog's powerful jaws. Downey transferred his right hand to the dog's throat, and began to work it, alternately squeezing and stroking. When his fingers had felt three gulps go down, he signaled the doctor with a nod to remove the bottle.

Fool capered gratefully when Downey put him down, leaping like a puppy to attract their attention. "You'd think he could read the label," Downey said. "That's prime whiskey."

Fool came down spraddle-legged after one of his leaps. He seemed to have lost his enthusiasm for showing off. He turned unsteadily and started to lope off in the direction of the alley in back of the hotel, where he had, by virtue of his size, first grabs at all scraps and table leavings. He looked to Downey like a dog who had just remembered something important that had to be taken care of before nap time.

Twenty feet away, he sat down. Ten seconds later, he lay down. When Downey walked over and lifted his hind end up by his tail, Fool did not wince—and this dog was a pure fool about having his tail touched.

"Be damned!" Lavoey muttered. "Who could've done it, and why? It beats me."

"It don't beat me," Downey said darkly.

CHAPTER 14

Rather than face Clytie, he ate at Tong Ti's, with Jerome Follansbee, who came foraging there to avoid having to eat formally with Ben Chase and his wife. The banker had heard about Charley Noble's mishap, but he failed to put two and two together. His only concern was to catch the evening Flyer back to Curtin, to be there when—and if—the money train reached there.

His attitude toward Downey was deferential, whereas Clytie's was bound to be critical. *She* would not be put off by any theory about Charley being the innocent victim of a dire plot to poison Downey. She knew Downey too well, had been too smitten by that virile mustache, and was too sensitive to the competitive lines of force between the two men. She did not mind two such men vying for her at all.

As he listened to Follansbee prattling about Chesty Bob Nylander, Downey wondered how Clytie would take it if Charley scalped himself before getting into bed with her. Would she shriek with surprise and dismay? Suppose a man had false teeth that he had to take out and put in a glass of water first, or a glass eye that he might lose in a tussle in the shucks? Or would a man with Charley's physical gifts blind them to everything else?

He had Tong Ti fill a tight-lidded syrup pail with black coffee, and offered to walk as far as the courthouse with Follansbee. "I've got a prisoner coming out of a bender about now. He'll need this," he said.

"That's very thoughtful of you," said Follansbee.

The bare-boned truth came out before Downey had time to

think. "Well, I been there myself, Jerry. Nobody gets treated worse than a cowboy when the fall roundup is over. When they still need men, it's, 'Come right in, son, make yourself to home!' Nothing's too good for you then. But when the job runs out, all they want to see is your back going down the trail. Many's the time I'd've shot up the town myself, only I didn't have this feller's nerve."

The banker caught hold of Downey's thick arm with his frail old hand. "You're a remarkable man, Rodge. I mean to see that Lord Dunconan makes your acquaintance. I want him to know one truly fine example of the frontier lawman."

It was the ultimate tribute but it left Downey unstirred. They shook hands and went their separate ways. In the jail, Joe Ogren lay on his stomach on his bunk, hands still tied behind him, eyes half open, face green. He shifted just enough to see who had come to the barred door, and then began cursing Downey and all he represented in a dull, hoarse, hopeless voice.

Joe was an easy man to detest at best, and at worst he stirred more than ordinary pity in the shamed and guilty Downey. "Get up off your bed, dummy, and come over here and let me untie you," Downey told him. "I've got some black coffee for you, just what you need."

"I don't want no black coffee," Joe said, but he stumbled to his feet and tottered over to where he could turn his back and let Downey cut the rope that bound him.

"I'll stir up the fire and put it on to heat some more. You'll want it soon, if you don't now."

Ogren turned, rubbing his numb hands together. "What'll I get for this, about six months' shoveling snow?"

"I don't know. I ain't the judge."

"What did you write down for my crime?"

"I'll have to see what Monte put down. Wait." Downey went in and consulted the ledger. Monte had not entered Joe's arrest at all, which was typical. "You ain't charged with nothing yet," Downey reported in a loud voice as he stirred up the fire. "You was shooting at everybody in town. That's several cases of attempted murder. You're lucky if you don't go to the pen."

"I don't give a damn. A poor man hasn't got a chance."

"Not much, although I been in your fix many's the time. Could you eat something?"

"Christ, no, especially jail grub."

"I'll get you something from Tong Ti's. He had some good applesauce. That lays easy on your stomach after you get a little coffee in you."

"You aim to feed me up good before you send me to the pen for attempted murder."

The fire was roaring. Downey dropped the poker. He went to the door to the cellblock. "Joe, you worthless bastard, you ain't even worth trying for murder. I think maybe what I'll do is charge you with drunk and disorderly, and get you a floater out of town."

"What if I won't go?"

Downey grunted loudly. "You'll go, all right."

"I mebbe could do with some coffee, at that. I've got just a splitter of a headache."

"It'll get worse, too, before it gets better. Let me fill a cup up for you."

He had to reach the cup through the bars and hold it for Joe to drink, so shaky were Joe's hands. It was the usual even-money bet whether he would keep his coffee his for a moment or two, but then he seemed suddenly to revive.

"You mean it about that applesauce, Sheriff?"

"Sure. You wait here."

"Now where did you expect me to wait?"

Downey could not help breaking into a grin. "You ain't entirely hopeless, Joe, if you can joke it up in your fix. Be right back."

He returned, just as the Flyer was pulling out of town, with another syrup pail containing more than a quart of applesauce. There was always a spoon in Downey's desk, and Joe had recovered to the point where he could feed himself. He had sense enough to eat slowly, waiting until he was sure one bite would stay down before taking another.

"Raw tomatoes fresh out of the garden are good after a drunk," he said, "but this applesauce beats them all holler. You live and learn, don't you?"

"Some people do. Other'ns just live."

Silence, while Joe gagged down a few more bites. He handed the spoon and pail back to Downey, and then leaned against the bars, supporting his weight mostly on the hands that gripped them. He was a big, ugly hulk, he smelled rancid, and his bloodshot eyes burned out of his haggard, unshaven face with the fire of fury.

"You never had a decent word for me before, Sheriff. Why are you treating me so good now?"

"Because I feel sorry for you, you dumb son of a bitch. Because I don't want my county to get a bad name with good cowboys. I want a good man who is looking for a job to know the dice ain't loaded against him here. If he thinks he's going to get drunk and shoot up the town afterward, he'll find out just like you did that he ain't going to do no such thing. Man, I been a cowboy all my life! There's nothing you can tell me about it."

Downey warmed to his subject, feeling some of the guilt and shame go out of him as he faced, at long last, some of the facts that had been too close to him to be seen clearly before this. The humiliation of playing the fool when he thought that Charley Noble was Chesty Bob, and the sick fear of losing Clytie to Charley, forced him to confess—in his own soul, at least—things he had always denied before.

"Joe, we all got to live together in this damn wild country. The poor man today is a rich man tomorrow, for all anybody knows, and the rich man today can go broke tomorrow. That's why everybody looks the same to me. I can't be bothered to pick on you! I'm too busy, and what would I have against you anyway, goddamnit?"

Joe began weeping gently, girlishly, letting the tears course down his big, ugly slab of a face. It was a moment before he could control himself enough to speak.

"Sheriff, I'm going to tell you something you ought to know," he said brokenly.

Downey chuckled. "What can you tell me that I ort to know?"

"You know that feller you had in jail here, that Chet Wilson? The one that had his hair cut off clear to the skin. That got away on that fiddling-feller's horse."

Downey jerked as though feeling a rope go taut around his feet. "What about him?"

"Listen, that jail break was all sham! Them two was in it together, and so was that goddamn old prizefighter of a preacher."

"Tom Fink, the Camden Bulldog? What about him?" Downey reached between the bars and shook Ogren hard. "Out with it! What the hell you trying to tell me?"

"Them three is camped there in the brakes in Wes Dodge's creek bottom-land. They robbed a clothesline somewhere and—"

"I know about that. Get on with it!"

"And this Wilson feller has got a squaw's wig and an old purple dress—"

"The Widow Scheidert's. Everybody knows that dress."

"I seen him myself, capering around in it like a fool. They are planning some kind of a robbery and they wanted me to go in on it, but I said no, I never robbed nobody in my life," Ogren said virtuously.

The man he had had in jail as "Chet Wilson" was Chesty Bob Nylander!

Downey knew there was no mistake this time. The horse that Fiddler Feathers had ridden—the one with the 51 brand —was Chesty Bob's horse, the one he had bought when he worked for Lord Dunconan. Tom Fink, the Camden Bulldog, was a third member of the gang that was to pull off the train robbery that would make Jesse and Frank James second-raters, so long as the history of robbery was recounted.

What better place to learn a town at one's leisure than in jail, with the sheriff, his deputy, and the town constable to run one's errands? Downey felt cold all over as he tried to remember how much he and Louie Varden had said here in the office. Not much, the way he remembered it. But one word would be one too many, with Chesty Bob himself listening with his sharp fox ears in his cell.

"They're camped on Wes Dodge's place, Joe?"

"Well, by now, prob'ly not. They was fixing to move on, I think. They wouldn't've let me get away if they didn't have so much on their minds. They really was excited, Mr. Downey! I don't know what they—"

"No way to land on them in the night, I guess."

"No way in the world. Even if they was still camped there, how are you going to get through them willow-brakes in the dark?"

"But there's only three of them?"

"When I was there, yes. But they was talking about Lafe getting there on time, and where they'd meet Eddie and Zeb. Honestly, Mr. Downey, I just watched my chance and made a run for my horse, and got out of there."

"Lafe" would no doubt be Lafayette Bray, a good rider gone wrong some years ago. Downey had taken Lafe at his word when he said he was through with all that, after doing his year and a half in prison in Nebraska. Chesty Bob was a persuader, for sure. Eddie and Zeb would be the Wagner brothers, a pair of poison-mean little runts who would do anything for money except work for it. Downey had thought that they knew better than to fool around in his county.

Downey felt old and bewildered suddenly. When he caught himself wishing that Louie Varden would turn up, to take charge of things, he knew he was too far past his prime to handle the biggest opportunity of his career.

"Be right back, Joe," he said. "Anybody comes in here, I

want you to keep a shut mouth in your head about what you just told me. You say one word, and you go to trial on all the attempted-murder cases I can talk them into filing. And I'll have plenty of witnesses, too."

"Mr. Downey—Sheriff, sir—I won't say a word. The first decent treatment I had since I became a grown man," Joe blubbered.

Back to Tong Ti's, to find Lena Barrett working behind a counter that was almost empty. Lena was a good worker who kept things clean. Downey stopped at the end of the counter, just inside the door, and watched the grace and strength with which she wiped down the counter. Everything the girl did was like a slow, dreamy dance. She was deliberately not noticing him.

The girl did not stir him—no, not one iota. He found himself in a strange sort of mood in which he seemed to be able to stand aside and see what a delicious bundle she was, but without caring personally. He rapped sharply on the counter with his knuckles and got her attention.

"Oh, Mr. Downey, I didn't know you was there!"

"You know it now."

She came toward him swayingly, half afraid, half bold in the power she thought she possessed.

"Where's Monte?" he said curtly when she got there.

"To home, taking care of the baby. I reckon they're both sound asleep by now."

He declined to receive the message. "You go home and tell him to get dressed and get down to the office, and I mean right now! Don't make a lot of fuss—don't tell anybody—just tell him to bring a bait of grub and be fixed to work all night."

"Oh gee, Mr. Downey, Tong's asleep, and I can't leave here until—"

He hit the counter again, harder. "God*damn*it, will you get going? I'll stir Tong out."

The girl fled with a little yelp of terror. Downey stormed

back through the kitchen to Tong's room and pounded on the locked door.

"Tong, Tong! I had to send Lena home to take care of their kid. Rise and shine, there."

It was never necessary to draw Tong a picture. "Sure, Sheriff, just let me pull on my pants."

And now he had to face Clytie, and that damned barber, and maybe Jim Lavoey.

CHAPTER 15

Dr. Lavoey had his hat on, ready to leave Downey's house, when he arrived there. His eyes were still full of malevolent suspicion, but he could prove nothing and they both knew it.

"He'll live, Rodge, but the longer he stays awake, the better it will be. If you get worried about him during the night, be sure to call me."

"I won't be here."

"Then tell Clytie to call me."

"You tell her."

Downey pushed past him and went on into the kitchen, where he could smell fresh coffee, and browned and crusted beef pot-roasted in the cast-iron pot on top of the stove. Clytie's back was to him as she stirred the brown gravy. Charley Noble sat at the table, smiling foolishly. His teeth looked as big as grave-markers, without the mustache.

"It sure is a funny thing, Mr. Downey," he said.

"What is?"

"Seems to me I remember you drinking your drink, before I could drink mine, in fact."

"That puzzles me, too," said Dr. Lavoey.

"How could it?" said Downey. "You wasn't there."

"No," said the doctor, "but Charley remembers everything else quite clearly, clear up to the time he went asleep after you throwed him down in the barber chair. If he remembers that, how could he make a mistake about you drinking your drink?"

"I don't know. So you remember me throwing you into

your chair, do you, Charley? How fur did I throw you, clear across the room, or what?"

Charley grinned that silly, half-drunk grin of his. The chloral hydrate still had not worn off entirely. "Well now, not throwed me, maybe. You just grabbed me by the arm and swang me backward and—"

"Swang you, hell. You was rubber-legged. Maybe you two have got time to set around and puzzle things out, but I've got to be up all night. I better eat in a hurry and get out of here."

"I thought you'd et at Tong Ti's," said Clytie.

"I did, and it was a long time ago, and I want to eat again, woman."

She got plates out and slammed them down on the table, while Downey took a bar of soap, a towel, and the teakettle to go outside to wash. The hot water on his face felt good, because it was already a cold night and due to get colder. It was only a mild stimulant, however, and it was a time when he needed a big one.

Lavoey was gone when he came back into the house. He sat down at the table and filled his plate with potatoes that had been browned with the roast. Clytie gave him a chunk of beef with sweet fat on it, the way he liked it. He ate ravenously. No woman on earth could cook better than Clytie, and he had never appreciated it more.

Clytie commented that the doctor had said for Charley to eat lightly tonight. Thus, Charley had only two plates of meat, potatoes, and gravy, and one slab of pie from the gooseberries Clytie had canned earlier in the fall. He was a little uncertain in his handling of knife and fork at first, but he seemed to gather strength as he fed.

"A man in my condition should get up from the table feeling he could eat as much more as he's already et," Charley said, crossing his knife and fork neatly at last. He held out his cup for another cup of coffee.

"You never will sleep, after all that coffee," Downey grunted.

"Mr. Downey, I could set right here and go to sleep and sleep a year." Charley stroked his lewdly nude upper lip. "I was a little sore at you for shaving this off, at first, but I'm glad now that you did."

"You are, are you?"

"Yes. I figgered once, it averaged that it took me ten minutes in the morning and ten at night to take care of it. Then about twice a week I had to take about fifteen minutes to trim it. Now, twenty minutes a day is a hundred and forty a week, plus another half hour is a hundred and seventy. Or, in round numbers, a hundred and eighty. Three hours a week, that's a hundred and fifty hours a year—why, fifteen whole working days just to keep up a mustache! It just ain't worth it."

"You looked good with it. It went with your hair, Charley," Clytie said. "But you look fine without it."

Downey said nothing to reveal that Charley's hair was a wig—and neither, noticeably, did Charley. Clytie did not sit down to the table until Downey had risen. Charley went on grinning that dreamy grin and drinking that strong black coffee.

Downey went into the bedroom to dig out warmer socks, a rite that meant that winter had arrived, whatever the calendar said. Vivid in his mind remained the picture of Charley and Clytie at the table, cozy and pleased. It was a picture with no room for him, and at the thought he wanted to bury his face in his hands and weep.

The door opened and Clytie came in. He found he had long since changed socks and put his boots back on, but he was still sitting on the edge of the bed. Clytie carried a short candle, the light of which made her lovely.

"You sick or what, Rodge?" she said.

"No. No, I ain't sick. Just thinking."

"You got plenty to think about, too."

"Now, what do you mean by that?"

"Why did you cut off his mustache?"

"Why shouldn't I?"

"It was a mean thing to do. You got a real mean streak in you, Rodge. You done that because he likes me, that's all."

"Where is he?"

"He wanted to go for a walk. The doctor said the more he walked and the longer he stayed awake, the better it would be."

He stood up and settled his coat better on his shoulders. "Well," he said, and could think of nothing else to say. Neither did he want to go.

"Charley would run off with me if I wanted him to," Clytie said.

"You already talked it over, I see," he managed to say calmly, although he felt such murderous rage that he wanted to smash her back against the wall with his fist.

"No, of course not. What do you think I am, anyway? But a woman can tell."

"Oh, she can, can she? Well, do you want him to?"

"I honestly don't know," she said. She looked him straight in the eye.

Yesterday he had had two wives—now, it appeared, he had none, Bobby being divorced and Clytie on her way off with this bald-headed, bald-faced barber. He thought it over carefully as he finished buttoning his coat. It would not do to let them know that they had knocked the wind right out of him.

"There's nearly six hundred dollars in the bank. I could get six or seven hundred cash for this place—more, if I wanted to carry somebody's note. I could raise another three hundred on the cow and my horses and some guns I don't need. You came to me with nothing but an old faded dress and some underpants and a petticoat, but nobody in your goddamn family will ever be able to say that you left me the same way. A thousand dollars, Clytie—that's what I'll give you, and I won't throw your new clothes up to you because you made them yourself."

"You don't have to give me nothing. I hope I earned the clothes that—"

"A thousand in cash and anything else you want to take along," he cut in harshly. He stalked past her and out the bedroom door. Before closing it, he turned back for one last word.

"I hate to see you go, especially with that silly son of a bitch. But if that—if that's what you want—if that's what it takes to make you happy—just so you get out of town and don't disgrace me."

He closed the door on her firmly, left the house, and walked swiftly down to the courthouse. He could see by the yellow light in the high window of his office that Monte was on the job. He went into the stable and saw that Monte's horse was saddled, and so was his own. Their bridles hung on the saddlehorns. All the horses were munching on oats in the dark.

Monte did not know what emergency portended, but he was doing his best to be ready for it. Might be that he'd make something of Monte yet. He went into the courthouse, and as he walked down the short corridor to his own office he heard the mellifluous bray of Charley Noble's voice:

". . . wasn't trying to poison me, no, sir! I ain't got an enemy in the world. No, sir, somebody found out how Mr. Downey and me hid a bottle, and it was *him* they was after. They tried to poison *our sheriff*, and if you ask me who done it—"

He walked in and said to the roomful of loafers, "Nobody asked you, Charley. You're supposed to be out walking. The rest of you get the hell out of here."

They bolted, all but Charley. Charley stood there with tears in his eyes and his toupee a little askew, holding out his big, soft, pink hand—the gentlemanly hand of a barber, silken-surfaced and perfumed for caressing. The hardest job Downey could remember was taking it; but take it he did.

"Now what the hell is this for, Charley?"

"I just want to pay my respects to our sheriff, that makes it possible for the law-abiding to sleep in their homes in peace," Charley choked.

Downey freed his hand and clapped it down on Charley's head. "Straighten your goddamn wig up. You go around looking like that, and everybody in town is going to know you wear one."

He got rid of Charley. Monte was looking at him, half excited, half fearful. Downey dropped his voice. "Monte, can Joe Ogren shoot?"

"Sober, he's a peach with a rifle. Many's the time I hunted with him. I reckon he can get by with a six-gun, too. Drunk, like today, he couldn't hit the broad side of a barn."

"Will he stand fire? You know him better than I do. Is he game, or will he lose his head if somebody shoots back?"

"I never been in no trouble like that with him, but my judgment is, Mr. Downey, I'd sooner have Joe beside me than anybody I know. Trouble's his middle name. I notice you untied him."

"Yes. Bring him in here, untied."

Monte leaped to obey. Downey himself kicked two chairs to the side of his desk and then locked the door. Monte and Joe watched him wonderingly as they took their seats. Downey sat down in his swivel chair.

"Monte, Joe is going to tell us about three prime bastards that you and me know very well, because they have plumb made us look like jackasses. Go ahead, Joe."

Joe told his story in the straightforward manner that left Downey in no doubt as to its truth. He was equally sure that there was nothing they could do tonight to gather the gang in. He could only organize a defense that would stand on its arms until it was attacked, and Monte and Joe must be the heart of it. The thought was not a cheerful one.

"What neither one of you know," he said when Joe had finished, "is that the UP puts a money car on one of its trains every month, for the banks along the line. Tomorrow's the day for this one."

"I see," Monte said softly. "And you figger these three aim to stick it up, do you?"

"I know damn well they do, because that shave-headed one in the dress, the one we had in jail under the name of Chet Wilson, is Chesty Bob Nylander."

Monte gasped. Joe Ogren merely narrowed his eyes and said, "I wondered about that myself, Mr. Downey. Any man that brags he's going to beat the Jameses' record is *loco*, and if you seen that galoot frolicking around in that dress and that wig, you'd know he was just that crazy. It gave me the creeps."

"Joe," Downey said, "you ain't as ignorant as you act sometimes. Now, the question is, who is in town that we can count on to stand up to these people? We're going to need help."

"There's three of them and three of us, Mr. Downey."

"Chesty Bob may be crazy, but not crazy enough to try to rob a train in *my* town with only two men. The others'll probably just be saddle bums. Chesty Bob and the fiddler and the Camden Bulldog—they're the ones that'll count. But any man with a gun in his hand can kill somebody. I want somebody that can kill him back. I wish we could get out to Hugh Dean's place in time to get back with his boys, but no chance. Start thinking of people."

He wrote the names down as Monte and Joe brought them up. Most of them could be discarded without much second thought. There just were not many young fighting men in a civilized town like Hillary.

Erik Sontag was an old soldier and could arm himself. What was more important, if any possibility existed that his own money was in danger, Erik would fight to the death. Tong Ti had no reputation as a fighting man, but he was a marksman, owned guns, and impressed all three as having all the nerve he needed. When Downey suggested one-legged Miller Mahaffey, the other two nodded: No question about old Miller having guts.

Buster Jacques, who worked for Sontag in hardware, and would at least know which end of a gun to point at you. Frank Barr, who milked a few cows, raised popcorn, and did a little blacksmithing, was cool to Downey for stealing his best milk customer, the Sontags. But he was an old soldier who would do his part. And Mike Dooley, the shoemaker and harness man, would feel hurt if left out of a fight.

"Then there's Charley Noble, if he's in shape," Joe Ogren said in the hoarse voice of a man who has been too long drunk.

"Yes, we need Charley," said Monte.

In all decency, Downey could not reject Charley. Neither could he let himself hope that Charley would get his bald head shot off. Downey swore Joe Ogren in as a deputy, and left him in charge of the jail. He sent Monte off to summon the others. He went himself, with lead in both heart and feet, to his own house, in search of Charley Noble.

His own front door was locked, and he could not bring himself to pound on it. He went around to the kitchen, and found it locked, too. There was a lamp burning in the kitchen, behind drawn blinds. He rapped on the door.

"Who is it?" came Clytie's voice.

"Who'd you think it is?" he growled.

She opened the door carefully. "Why did you come around back?"

"Because the front door was locked."

"You're just in time to empty the tub, if you got the time."

She was in her long nightgown, the winter one that she postponed wearing as long as possible. It smelled of the lilac sachet of summer storage. She was just out of the bathtub, and was drying her long, heavy hair. Her face glowed with such enchantment that he had to look away.

He carried the tub out, emptied it, took time to rinse it at the pump, and hung it on the nail on the side of the house. When he came back in, Clytie was just starting to braid her hair.

"Where's Charley?"

"Why," she said, "I don't know. He ain't been back since he went for his walk. He said he reckoned he'd had enough sleep to do him till spring, like a bear."

"This don't look much like running off together."

"What?"

He could only stare at her. She finished the braid, tied it nimbly, started on another. Slowly, the color mounted in her tawny cheeks as she stared back in a strange sort of defiance.

"Running off together—who? For God's sake, Rodge, I only said he would. Not that I would."

"You—you said you liked him."

"I—I do."

He had a sudden memory of old Andy Bagley, whom he had ridden with for nearly two years when he was—oh, in his late twenties. Andy had been old enough to be his father, and in some ways he acted like one. Andy was a one-eyed man with a glass eye that didn't quite match his good one. Or fit very well, either. Andy had bought it from an undertaker in El Paso, and had learned from him how to take care of it.

Every night he took it out and washed it carefully, and slept without it. In the morning, he would pick it up and put it in his mouth while he dressed, to warm it up and get it slick enough with spit to pop into place. He felt naked without it, and yet that staring, immovable hazel pop-eye was twice as conspicuous as an eye-patch. The girls in the cribs used to charge him extra because of that goddamn misfit eye.

Poor Andy, who so wanted to be loved, who tried so hard to be a ladies' man, and who was such a good friend when Downey needed one! He had not thought of Andy for—

"But I like a lot of people," Clytie was saying. "In fact, there ain't many people I don't like. But if you remember, when you asked Pa if I could marry you, I said I didn't even *like* you. And I didn't. And in some ways, there's still a lot of things you do that I don't like one bit. But lord, Rodge, you don't *like* your husband. You—you—you—"

She either could not or would not say it. She made him. He clutched her arms and smelled the lilac sachet and the clean skin and damp hair.

"You mean—you mean—you love me, Clytie? *Me?*"

"Well, Rodge, you *are* a fool! Why'd you think I married you, and lived all these years with you? Oh, Rodge, if it could only be like that first night on the train—not all the time, but once in a while! Oh, if you could only not be so—so—"

"I won't be anymore. I love you, Clytie!"

"Not now, not now! Oh Christ, Rodge, what if that damn pest of a Charley—"

He swooped her up in his arms and headed for the bedroom, stopping only to lock the back door again.

CHAPTER 16

At daylight, he stirred the depot agent out of bed, hurrying on foot through a cold and silent town. He did not feel tired. He did not know what the word meant. He was affable but bossy, clapping the agent on the back as he gave him stern orders to get the information on all trains moving on the division.

Within forty minutes he was able to report to his yawning posse that crowded his little office. Only Charley Noble was alert. He was red-eyed and needed a shave, but over and over he said that he still felt caught up enough on sleep for a smart spell.

"The money train is due in here at ten after eleven. Usually it has right-of-way over everything on the line, but today there's some kind of a damn special coming from the East. So the money train has to go into the hole for it here," he said.

"What's 'go into the hole'?" someone asked.

"It has to take a side-track and wait until the special clears. I only wish I knowed if Chesty Bob had anything to do with it."

"Bet you a dollar he did," somebody said.

"It don't make our job no easier. Ben Chase, the damn fool, has got a lot of cash in the bank. Chesty Bob will know about that, like he does everything. Question is, where'll he hit first, the bank or the train?"

"The train!" said Joe Ogren. "That's all that fool has thought about for years."

"But," said Downey, "even if you're Chesty Bob, a train robbery ain't no Ladies Aid meeting. Me, I'd hit the bank about a quarter of eleven. Clean it out hard and fast, hit the train when it comes in, and then ride like hell. He's got to get away clear, remember."

"Maybe that's what the special train is for," Monte suggested.

"I thought of that. I wish I had a dozen more men, to make sure that don't work."

There was a knock at the door, which Monte opened. It was the depot agent, with a telegram that was not for Downey. "But the way things is, Sheriff," the agent said, "I reckon you ort to see it first."

Downey read the wire and then handed it around for the others. It was addressed to the livery stable, and it said:

REQUEST SMARTEST TEAM AND BEST TURNOUT MEET SPECIAL TRAIN ARRIVING ELEVEN FIVE STOP DO NOT FAIL.
J. L. TINDALL CONDUCTOR SPCL TRAIN

"Thanks." Downey handed the telegram back to the agent. "Tell him to do the best he can. The sorrel buggy team and the funeral carriage, I reckon."

The agent departed. There was much discussion of the special train and the fine rig that had been ordered to meet it. Downey cut it short, to lay out his plan of battle. He would concentrate on the bank, but he would leave hidden riflemen —the best long-gun shots he had, Tong Ti and Miller Mahaffey—where they could cover the bank too.

But they were under orders not to interfere at the bank until he gave them a long whistle. Using their own judgment, they were to move down toward the depot, still in hiding, to cover it, should gunfire break out there.

"If they drop me, Monte's in charge. Anybody want to object?"

"I don't know as I'm the man for the job," Monte said. He looked down at the floor.

"You can whistle like a steam engine. Let's hope that's all

you have to do. Now, everybody go take their places. Stay out of sight! I'll be in plain sight myself, keeping people off the street all I can. We don't want to spook nobody, but we don't want nobody getting in the line of fire, either. Let's go!"

They left by ones and twos, as casually as they had gathered together. It was the season when men were gathering game for the family table, and those who carried rifles and shotguns were not conspicuous. Downey was the last to leave. Before locking the office he put his "everyday" gun in his holster and shoved his "dress" .45 into his hip pocket. He carried one of his favorite weapons, a Remington .30-30 carbine, a lever-action gun that had never let him down.

He had no trouble clearing the streets. He did not have to explain anything to anyone. "Afraid we might have some bad trouble, and I don't want nobody hurt," was all he had to say. It was comforting to see how people, true folks all, respected his opinion and took his orders.

How lucky he was! His blundering life could have ended with him on the junk heap, or a misfit like poor Andy Bagley. Instead, here he was, sheriff and a leader of the people, about to face the sternest test a sheriff and leader could face. And he had no fear of the outcome. There was a spring in his step, peace in his mind, peace in his heart.

Downey found his own command position on top of the privy in the town wagon lot. He rolled an up-ended barrel to the side of the privy, to make it easier to scramble up and down. From either the bank or the depot, he would be seen indistinctly against a background of scrub pines, yet his own view was just about perfect.

Every now and then he got down, carrying the .30-30, to ask some citizen to get off the street. Usually it was a woman on her way to a store. He tipped his hat to each, and gave each the absent smile of a very busy man.

Ben Chase got to the bank ten minutes early. If the empty streets puzzled him, nothing in his manner showed it. He unlocked the door and went in, and Sis Bell, the assistant cashier, was not more than a minute behind him. Sis had worked for Ben's father. She was a muscular spinster whose true, powerful alto required the best of any three sopranos in the church choir. When Sis was at the teller's grille, you sighed with relief when she changed your ten-dollar bill without question. Somehow she had you sure it was counterfeit by the time your turn came.

The minutes dragged into hours. At a little after ten, Downey saw Judge Dilham pacing slowly past the bank, on his way to the post office. Downey dropped to the barrel and then to the ground, and intercepted the judge.

"Hidy, Judge. Wish you'd take the other way home, and not take too long socializing in the post office," he said.

"Why? That's a tiresome climb." The judge saw the .30-30 in Downey's right hand, carried at the ready. "Something doing this morning?"

"I sure hope so."

"That railroad detective's tip coming true?"

"I ain't saying no more. You might end up with some customers in your court, and you ain't getting no more chances to lecture me like you did once."

The judge smiled, recalling the time he had scolded Downey, then in his first year in office, for having talked to him about a case before making an arrest. "Very well, we will not compromise the integrity of the court. How did you sleep last night, Rodge?" he said.

"I didn't. How about you?"

"The same. I won't keep you. Good luck!"

The judge speeded up his pace, and, after leaving the post office, cut across high, steep lots to get home. Watching him from the top of the privy, Downey felt a surge of something more than respect for the old codger. He felt real affection for him, too.

A ramshackle covered wagon pulled by a pair of good sorrel mare-mules came creaking down the road in the distance. There was a water bucket slung under the end of the tongue, a crate of chickens under the wagon bed. More shiftless emigrants on their way to—where? Oregon, they thought. They had the mules for it, but not the wagon. They'd end up riding the mules over the Continental Divide, or selling them to get back home.

He looked at his watch: ten fifty-two. He stood up and put his fingers in his mouth to whistle lightly. He saw several of his men stick their heads out in response, among them Charley Noble. He pointed to Charley and then to the covered wagon.

"Keep them out of the wagon lot, Charley. They can feed and water somewhere else," he called.

Charley propped his shotgun against a wall, out of sight, and went to meet the wagon. The lanky, bearded old driver gave Charley a long, tiresome argument, but he turned his rig around at last, with much backing and geeing and hawing, and went creaking back the way he had come. Downey watched him tie a block beyond the bank, wrapping his lines securely before getting down from the wagon seat. He took the bucket from the end of the tongue and headed for Bill Peterpy's well.

The sound of shod hooves in another direction turned Downey's head. He saw the livery barn's funeral rig heading for the depot to meet the special. The fine old carriage had been polished to a satiny black. The two sorrels were getting a little old now, but they could still step out smartly for a few miles. Bill Grogan himself was at the lines, clean-shaven and in a new shirt.

Again Downey consulted his watch. It was just eleven, and he should have been getting nervous and sweaty and on edge. He was none of these things. Whatever they do, he told himself, I'll handle it. . . .

Again he turned, to see the old emigrant groaning as he toted a full bucket of water to the mules. Somewhere, then, he heard running horses. He got off his haunches to his knees in time to see two runaway horses, saddled and bridled, and with the reins tied up around their necks, come around the curve in the road from which the emigrant wagon had appeared.

Not a hundred feet behind them came a rider swinging a rope—a good man he was, too, with a big loop and every inch of that long rope under control. Downey stood up and shouted.

"Charley! Stop them horses—turn them some other way—get them to hell off the street."

Charley again put his shotgun down and ran out, waving his arms. The horses broke back when they saw him. The rider's loop dropped neatly over the head of one. It came taut. The horses stopped fighting. The other runaway gave up and let Charley catch his reins.

"Goddang crazy cayuses, and the damned old fool that expects a man to do everything," the cowboy said, leaning out of the saddle to take the reins of the runaways. He was almost weeping in his rage.

Downey could hear Charley clearly: "Just get on out of here with them. You ort to have more sense than to let them get away from you in town. Get going!"

"What the hell you think I'm trying to do?"

Suddenly it was as though a veil had been ripped away from the whole innocent picture, to Downey. He saw the emigrant put the bucket down in front of one mule, and then the other. *Neither mule drank.*

What kind of overland traveler was it that watered his mules before he harnessed them, and then watered them again before noon on a cold day like today? And why had a strange rider let two saddled and bridled horses get away from him, only to be caught practically in front of the bank?

Just as Downey expected, a woman clambered out of the emigrant wagon, wearing a sunbonnet over a tangle of curls— and a faded purple dress. Downey stood up, put his fingers in his mouth, and whistled a blast so loud and piercing that it made his own ears ring.

"The woman, the woman—that's Chesty Bob! And that son of a bitch watering the mules is Fiddler Feathers. Up with your hands, you thieving bastards! You're all under arrest," he shouted.

The "emigrant" dropped the bucket of water and headed toward the bank. The "woman" reached into the wagon and handed him something that looked to Downey like five or six sticks of dynamite and some fuse. The "cowboy" with the "runaway" horses trotted smartly around the bank building, out of everybody's range.

Downey kept his eye on the "woman" as he dropped first to the barrel and then to the ground. He began running toward "her." Monte came out of hiding without being summoned, and fell into step beside him.

Fiddler, in his emigrant costume, vanished into the bank. Another man rolled out of the covered wagon, and another one, and then another. All carried sawed-off shotguns that made Downey's blood run cold.

Joe Ogren came out from behind a hayshed and sprinted to get between the "woman" and the bank. One of the men turned and fired one barrel of his sawed-off shotgun. Joe stumbled, clutched at his guts, and almost dropped his gun.

He went to his knees and brought up the gun, but even at this distance Downey could see the blood on his face. The "woman" who was Chesty Bob Nylander under that silly get-up pulled a .45 out of the bosom of "her" dress, and fired before Joe could. The slug caught Joe dead in the chest and threw him backward. He did not move.

Inside the bank, Sis Bell screamed a pealing alto scream. Mike Dooley and Frank Barr raced into view, heading for the back of the bank, as they had been ordered to do. Miller Mahaffey had Downey's own Springfield .45-70, but he was not staying out of sight according to orders. He had come stumping out on his wooden leg, the big gun held across his chest. Behind him came Buster Jacques, carrying a .45 so brand new that its blued steel glinted.

A slug ripped through Buster's lower leg and he toppled with a shriek. He kept rolling as two more shots pursued him. Miller lifted the .45-70 and fired almost from the hip, without sighting. Downey could not see the man who had shot Buster, but he heard his scream and heard it turn into a moan, all in a matter of seconds.

Downey waved Miller back, but the constable clacked the bolt of the Springfield and fed another huge slug into the chamber. But he stood there and let Chesty Bob pick up her skirts—*his* skirts—and race into the bank.

Fiddler Feathers came out of the bank at a dead run, saw Downey, and scrambled for his gun. Downey fired as he ran, two shots. He saw the first one go high, barking the fiddler's shoulder without downing him, but the second one got him in the ribs. Fiddler was turned halfway around, but he fell with the gun in his hand and he got off two shots before Downey fired a third time.

He knew that Feathers was dead by the way he fell. There was shooting in back of the bank, too. Beside Downey, Monte was taking his time, firing back under fire like a veteran infantryman. He was so white he looked blue, but, scared as he was, his nerve was holding fine.

A man dropped his empty sawed-off shotgun and whirled to face Downey, going for his .45. Tom Fink, the Camden Bulldog! They fired almost at the same time, Downey dropping to his knee as he squeezed the trigger. He felt Fink's slug slide past him. He saw his own slug half tear the Camden Bulldog's right arm off at the elbow. Fink sat down and held his right arm with his left and screamed.

Inside the bank, Sis Bell screamed again. Mike Dooley came running out from behind the bank. Downey, still on one knee as he reloaded, heard Mike shouting his name.

"Rodge, Rodge! Ben Chase wants to talk to you. Hold your fire. He's coming to the door."

"Hold your fire at the bank, everybody," Downey commanded. "Anybody moves anywhere else, get him."

The bank seemed to be full of gunsmoke. Through it, hands held so high it must have hurt him, came the banker, Ben Chase. He was in the doorway when someone behind him called an order in a high, giggling voice.

"That's fur enough. They can hear you from there, Mr. Chase. If they cain't, they can come closer."

Downey knew that voice. That was Chesty Bob, who had enjoyed life in Downey's jail under the name of Chet Wilson. Ben stopped as though hauled back by a tight wire. He licked his lips.

Down near the depot, an engine hooted. Steam hissed as the engineer opened his cylinder cocks to make a showy stop. Ben Chase was blathering away, but the engine was making too much noise. Without getting off his knees and making a target of himself, Downey called back:

"Speak up, Ben. Nobody can hear you with that damn locomotive making all that racket."

Mike Dooley had to speak up for him. He cupped his hands around his mouth and shouted: "He says you got to let them through. They're taking him and Sis Bell with them. Rodge, that son of a bitch inside there said he'll blow the bank up with everybody in it before he'll let us take him."

Downey dared a glance back at the train. It was the special from the East, with only two cars on it. From one was descending a burly, well-dressed man that Downey recognized even at this distance. His son! Edmund D. Rodgerson, as he called himself. He turned on the platform to give his hand to a portly woman in taffeta and furs, who descended the steps like a duchess.

Oh my God, Downey thought, that's Bobby. . . .

CHAPTER 17

Someone was peering around the rear corner of the bank building, braying at the top of his voice: "They got dynamite inside, Rodge. Can you hear me? Dynamite!"

Downey stood up and shouted, "Shut up, shut up, *shut up!*" The fool shut up. Downey cocked both hands on his hips and faced Ben Chase.

"What's the matter with you, Ben?"

"Rodge, they want to get away," Ben quavered. "If you let them, nobody'll get hurt."

"And if I don't?"

"They got six sticks of dynamite fused, ready to blow us all to hell and gone. Rodge, money ain't everything. I'll make the bank's losses good out of my own funds. Let 'em go!"

"With all the money in the bank?"

"Not all," Ben said piteously.

"They're leaving you the silver, I reckon, and taking everything else. The 'bearer' bonds, too? How much altogether? About thirty thousand?"

Ben moaned. "I don't know exactly. About that. But I *said* I'd make it good. That's a promise, Rodge."

"All you men heard Ben say that, now. He said he'd make the losses good," Downey shouted. "But I want to hear Chesty Bob say it himself. I don't make no deals with anybody but him, Ben."

Ben whimpered something over his shoulder. A palaver that Downey could not hear went on and on and on. A shadowy figure appeared inside the bank, sheltered by Ben Chase's body. Then Downey heard the rollicking voice he had learned to know so well while "Chet Wilson" was in his jail:

"You there, Sheriff Downey. I'll trust you, old-timer, but nobody else, you hear?"

"Go on," Downey called back.

"You shuck your gun and step back two steps, and stay right there. The rest of your men, I want them to go over and throw their guns in the wagon, where we can see 'em from the side winder. They line up then, flat on their bellies, while we come out. Got that?"

"I got that."

"Listen, old sheriff—there'll be one man covering me with a Winchester as we go. If you think he can't shoot that gun, just try your luck! That's the deal, or I blow up the bank."

"You'll blow yourself up, too."

A high, wild giggle. "I don't reckon so. I think you're going to take my deal."

Downey lifted his coat to unbuckle his holster. We sure thinned them out, he thought, if they's only two left. . . . He lowered gun and holster to the road.

"You hear? Do as he says!" he shouted. "Don't nobody take chances, hear me? Remember, Sis Bell is inside there, too."

He was fairly sure that Charley Noble, behind him, could see the new .45 in his hip pocket. He only hoped the fool would know better than to give it away. He took two backward steps, and waited.

The others came out swiftly, tossed their guns into the covered wagon, and lay down in the street on their faces. Miller Mahaffey was weeping openly with shame. From where Downey stood, he could see four dead bodies, all bank robbers who had been so damn sure they could beat Chesty Bob at his own game.

"You got your deal, Nylander," Downey called. "Come on out and get it over with."

"Don't nobody make a move," Nylander cried. "Here we come."

He had shucked the dress and was in ragged Levi pants and an old sweater. In his left hand, he carried a valise weighted down with thirty thousand dollars, give or take a few thousand. The back door of the bank slammed distantly, and another man came around the building. He was carrying a Winchester model 70 and leading two horses. The rifle would throw a .44 slug a quarter of a mile—if you could shoot it that well.

One of the horses was the fine gelding with the 51 brand that Fiddler Feathers had ridden into town, the horse bred on Lord Dunconan's place. It was fighting the bit and frothing at the mouth with nervous terror, after all the shooting. Chesty Bob took its reins and tried to haul himself into the saddle, holding the valise.

The terrified horse shook him off. Chesty dug in his heels and turned to squall at the man with the big Winchester: "Trade horses with me. This son of a bitch won't stand for the valise."

The man with the Winchester held both horses while Chesty mounted the second one. To Downey, it was like standing aside and watching a bit of action whose end he had already seen before. He was just that sure what Chesty Bob was going to do; and he did it.

"Get that son of a bitch of a sheriff!" Chesty screamed as he sank in his spurs.

The rifleman held the 51 horse's reins in his left hand and swiveled his body to fire the Winchester from the hip, from no more than twenty feet away. Downey calmly plucked the new .45 from his hip pocket. He saw the look of stupid amazement flit across the rifleman's face as he saw the .45.

They fired at the same time, and Downey felt his left leg buckle under him. But he saw where his slug smashed into the rifleman's stomach. The man dropped the rifle and went to his knees, fouling the reins of the wild 51 horse in his own armpit as he twisted in agony on the ground. He did not know when the horse stepped on him, or that his own dead weight was what presented Downey with the horse.

Downey knew how to approach a frightened horse. He got hold of its bridle and brought the curb chain up snug. He hooked his toe under the dead rifleman and turned him over, freeing the reins. He knew he could not trust his leg when he looked down and saw the blood spreading over his thick thigh, but the pain did not come until he had hauled himself into the saddle.

Now, he thought, it's just between Chesty Bob Nylander and me, and that's just the way I want it. . . . He heard another locomotive whistle, and saw an eastbound train rocking slowly up the uneven passing track. It was the money train, going "into the hole" for the special, and swinging from the steps of the first passenger car was a white-faced Union Pacific detective, Louie Varden.

Chesty Bob whirled his horse toward the depot as the money train barred his way. The crowd from the special scattered, shrieking, as he flailed his horse down the cinder platform. The engineer of the special yanked on his whistle. The deafening blast, exploding almost in the horse's ear, sent it out of control again.

Back down the platform it came. Downey's son was the only one in that crowd keeping his head. Downey saw him drop to his knees behind a stack of freight, and take a small pistol from his pocket. It cracked twice, and Downey grinned. Got to teach that boy to lead his target, he told himself, as both shots missed. . . .

There was no escape across the tracks. Chesty Bob spun the horse once more and headed back through the town, with Downey after him. And Downey was sure now that he had the better horse. In fact, he wondered if he had ever been on a horse as good as this one with the 51 brand, as he felt the power in those long, reaching legs. He would run Chesty Bob down in less than a mile.

Lena Barrett came out of Tong Ti's to see the excitement. She stood there and watched Chesty Bob race toward her, with her hands over her mouth like a fool. Chesty pulled up beside her and grabbed one of her wrists. For an instant his horse was again out of control, with both of his hands occupied.

Chesty Bob might not be as brainy an outlaw leader as he fancied himself, but he was hell on wheels when it came to saving his loot and his own hide. He drove his heels into the horse's flanks, and Lena had to pull herself up behind the saddle or fall under the horse's feet. Past the bank he went, where there were men who had recovered their guns but who dared not shoot because of Lena.

The town vanished behind them. The road squirmed around sharply, to reach across a creek at its narrowest point. Downey was so close by then that his horse's hooves picked up the drum of the planks before Chesty Bob's horse was off the other end. Downey could see Lena's wildly rolling eyes and the utter pallor of her face when she heard him coming behind them and looked back.

A hundred yards onward, and Chesty Bob dropped the valise in the road, spun the horse, and yanked out his .45. He pressed the muzzle against Lena's ribs and shouted, "Hold it there, you sheriff, you! Keep your distance or I cut this woman in two."

Downey hauled in his horse. He could feel his foot growing wet with his own blood in his boot, and he knew that no man could last long with that kind of wound in him.

"What good will it do you to kill her, Nylander? Better come along peaceable, and see if the judge won't count that in your favor," he said.

"Get off your horse," Nylander said.

Now Downey knew that he was crazy. You had to handle a

crazy man different than you did a sane one. This old smart-aleck had come to the end of his boasting and bragging. Instead of beating the James Boys' record, he had to talk an old country sheriff into letting him get away with his life and his loot. By the look in his eye, he would take Lena with him in a shoot-out, out of pure wild rage and shame and disappointment.

"Please, Mr. Downey, do what he says," Lena said. "Please, don't make him shoot me!"

Chesty Bob grinned. "You heard her, Mr. Downey, sir. Get off that horse, and help me up on it and hand me that money. Onliest way you two is going to live."

"Chesty," said Downey, "I got a better deal for you. Let's you and me split what's in that valise. You ain't got all day, so make up your mind quick."

Nylander stared at him, and then down at Lena. "But what about her?"

"What about her? The hell with her! You throw your gun down and I'll throw mine down. I'll hide my half of the money in the weeds, here, and you take your half and ride like hell. I'll worry about her."

"But hell, Sheriff—"

A wave of nausea like a blow in the stomach hit Downey, and he knew he was losing blood faster than he could afford to lose it. The pain was nothing. He had never felt pain like this before, but he had felt every other humiliation and disappointment. He could stand the pain, but he could not stand fainting from loss of blood, and losing this last showdown with Chesty Bob.

He said, "Chesty, there'll be a posse on your tail so fast, you might as well hang yourself. Can't you see that it's half or nothing? Get off that horse fast, and I'll get off mine. Throw your gun down, and I'll throw mine down. Goddamnit to hell, you know my word! You was in my jail long enough to know I don't lie to nobody."

"All right," Chesty said, "I'll put this woman down, and I want her to go over to the side of the road and not get between us. Then we both get off, and walk towards each other. And when you give the word, we throw our guns down and divide the money."

Downey merely nodded. Chesty Bob shoved an elbow into her body and muttered, "Get down. Get the hell out of the way, woman!"

Lena hit the ground hard, on her bottom. She did not bother to get up, but scrambled to the side of the road on all fours.

Downey had to grit his teeth against both pain and weakness to be able to swing out of the saddle like a well man. He kept a sharp eye on Chesty Bob, and had time for a piercing regret that so much limber youth and strength had to be wasted on the likes of him. He could hear his foot go *squish-squish-squish* in his own bootful of blood as they began walking toward each other.

They were no more than ten feet apart. "Hold it!" Downey said.

They stopped, facing each other. It was a good feeling, to be in command this way, to know that he had cornered this Chesty Bob Nylander on a country road after he had driven the banks and peace officers of four states mad for five years.

"My gun's in my hip pocket. I'm going to count to three, Nylander, and then we'll both take our guns out and let them dangle plumb out of our hands. Not even raise them, you got that?"

"I got it, Mr. Downey."

"All right, then. One . . . two . . . *three!*"

Slowly, carefully, he took the new "dress" .45 from his hip pocket, keeping it low, keeping it pointed toward the ground. Chesty Bob matched him move for move. On the count of three, Bob let his gun fall to the ground.

Downey tipped his up and shot Chesty Bob in the chest. He saw the look of outrage cross the outlaw's face, just as the big slug blew his heart to pieces. A man could almost hear Chesty Bob telling his deluded, riffraff following, "Oh hell, don't worry none about that old fool sheriff. I tell you, I been in his jail! He's just an old country nobody."

Downey fired again, as Chesty Bob pitched forward, and caught him in the temple. Then Downey himself sat down. He had heard people say that everything had gone black, but this was not the case with him. Weakness made everything sort of blue-gray.

"Lena!" he said. "Hey, girl, come here."

She seemed dazed. "Huh, Mr. Downey?"

"You're a good rider. Take one of these horses and—no, first, throw that valise over to me. Then you get into town fast, and tell them to bring Doc Lavoey here. Tell them I'm losing blood fast, and like to die. But tell them first that I shot Chesty Bob Nylander dead."

"Oh, Mr. Downey, I can't, in a dress," Lena wailed. "What if somebody seen me?"

"Seen your bare hind end? Shit!" He choked on his own anger. "Woman, get in that saddle and ride! But first throw that valise to me. Hurry!"

The 51 horse had had the ginger run out of him. He let the girl catch him without trouble. She got up in the saddle, and her sleek, bare shanks were just as white and smooth and breathtakingly pretty as he had known they would be. He managed to get the pocketknife out of his pocket and open it. He hacked off the leg of his pants and found where the bullet had gone in. He could feel where it had gone out the back, but by now he was too weak and confused to see it, too. He got his handkerchief out, blessing Clytie because she always saw to it that he had clean ones, and wrapped it as tightly as he could around his thick leg, over both wounds.

The blue-gray color was growing deeper, and he was sick at his stomach and very, very tired. He put his head down on the valise that had thirty thousand dollars in it, and went peacefully to sleep on the cold road, with the cold wind blowing over his slack gray face.

CHAPTER 18

He knew when Doc swabbed the wound out by pulling a string through it with a wad of cloth on the end, because it hurt. But he did not know where he was, nor did he care much. It was a relief to go to sleep again in the middle of Doc's thick-fingered operation, and this time sleep was blackness, as people said.

He knew it was morning when he awakened because he could smell sausage frying and see the glitter of sun through the blinds. He was in his own bed, on his back, propped up on three pillows. In a corner on a wooden chair sat a man, sleeping. He had a red face and a bald red scalp, and it took Downey a moment to recognize Charley Noble.

He waited quite a while, until he was sure he was going to be able to get the words out.

"Charley," he said.

No answer. He waited and tried it again, a few minutes later.

"Charley!"

The fool opened his eyes. He leaped to his feet, yawning guiltily. "Why, you're awake, Mr. Downey," he said. "We been taking turns sitting up with you all night. There's a man here that came on the special train. Him and me has been sitting up with you."

"A man?"

Charley beamed. "By the name of Rodgerson. I reckon he must be some kind of a relation of yours, but he didn't say. Doc's having some breakfast. Clytie made some kind of a deal for half a hog yesterday, and she's getting the meat ready to smoke. I'll tell them you're awake, Mr. Downey."

You do that, Downey thought wearily. The doctor was the first one into the room. He felt Downey's pulse, meanwhile watching the hand of his watch spin around. "You are one tough old man, Rodge," he said. "I declare, I never seen a body recover pressure and heartbeat this fast."

"The money, Doc?"

"Ben got it all back. Every cent. Chesty Bob has been identified. We've had two wires from the governor about you, and one from Randy Crocker. He's coming in on the first possible train. Lord Dunconan is in town yet. So is Mrs. Rodgerson and her son—I assume they're kin of yours. The whole town has remained awake all night, Rodge, praying for you."

"Hell of a note," Downey said. "Nobody ever prayed for me before."

"You prob'ly never deserved it before."

Clytie came in, drying her hands on a fresh towel. She had her old timidness back, as though, having spoken up once or twice recently, it was a relief to be back in her place. He tried to lift his hand to her, but it just plain weighed too much.

All he could do was look at Doc until Doc got the message and went out. "Don't worry, Clytie. Keep him quiet and he'll be all right. He could still live to hang," Doc said as he went out.

Clytie came to the bedside. At his nod, she sat down and took his hand in both of hers. He smiled as best he could. She tried to smile back, and he knew not only that something was troubling her but what it was.

"That fellow," he said weakly. "He's my son."

"I knowed it the minute I seen him. He says his mother is here, too. Is she your—your wife, Rodge?"

He had to save up strength to whisper it. "Was, a long time ago. You go upstairs in the attic, hon, and look in that old trunk. There's a bunch of papers, and I think I throwed them right on top. Bring them down, and then you and my son come back in here."

He was asleep again before she was out the door. When he awakened, Clytie was standing beside the bed, with the papers in her hand. His son stood at the foot of the bed, smiling down at him. Downey did not speak. He glanced first at Clytie, then at the papers, then at his son. Silently Clytie handed over the papers.

His son, being a lawyer, did not fool around. He came to the decree of divorce, and read it swiftly, with a frown. He took it to the window to read it again, and to examine the certification at the foot of the document. When he turned back to Downey he was again smiling.

"I don't suppose you'll mind my taking the date and numbers from this, in case it becomes necessary for me to get a copy of it," he said.

"Take that one, if you want it," said Downey.

"No, it may become important to your wife, if not to you. This settles a number of questions, as I'm sure you know. But I want to assure you that my mother did not know this decree had been granted. In fact, I rather think the whole thing is illegal—if we could prove it at this time. I have a suspicion that there never was a hearing, but we would have only my mother's unsupported word for that. And she won't contest it."

"What will she do?" Clytie said, unexpectedly.

"Why, marry Lord Dunconan, I imagine. He has been after her for years, but she has never been able to come to the point of saying yes. In her heart, she never forgot my father. Now she must."

Clytie looked at Downey. "She wouldn't marry a lord because of you. Jesus, Rodge!"

"Well," he said uncomfortably, "she never did have real good sense."

His son laughed. He folded the papers up again and dropped them on the foot of the bed.

"I won't say goodbye—just so long, for now. I hope I can come back and see you again."

"Sure."

"You're a mighty lucky man, you know. Your wife is a wonderful woman. I'll have to hurry back now and talk to Mother. It's going to be painful. So now that I know you're going to get well, I probably shall not see you again this trip. But when you announce for lieutenant governor, I've got quite a few friends I'll want you to meet."

They shook hands—rather, Downey let his hang weakly while his son did the shaking. His son went out. Clytie sat down on the edge of the bed.

"That sneaky old Crocker is going to come here to see you. Judge Dilham has been here. He said they've already give up, and you're their candidate. Mebbe you should've give your first wife a chance to come back to you, Rodge. You don't want a plain old farm woman like me for a lieutenant governor's wife."

There was a real mob in the little house, making a racket fit to shake it down, keeping Clytie from her work in getting half a hog put up for the winter. She made as if to get up, but he caught her by the hand. He really had not that much strength; but she did not fight him.

"I ain't going to run for lieutenant governor," he said, "but that ain't why. You'd be just fine if I was President of the United States. But I wouldn't be that, either, if everybody in the world voted for me."

"Why not?"

He had to close his eyes and rest a moment. He opened them again. "All my life I been a cheat and a scoundrel, pretending to be what I wasn't. Now I really am what I claimed to be, and that's all I want the rest of my life."

"What's that?" She leaned over to kiss him on the forehead, and left her cheek against it for a moment.

"Sheriff for all the people," he said.